I0733963

The Room Where it Happened

Anne Louise Bannon

HH
Healcroft House, Publishers
Altadena, California

ISBN: 978-1-948616-50-8

Library of Congress Control Number: 2025909405

Contents

Acknowledgements

It seemed like such a silly writing prompt, and yet it was intriguing. "Write a story that begins, And this is the room where it happened."

This book came out of that prompt, which came about because of a journaling group that was formed by Los Angeles Public Librarian Barbara Birnbaum in the spring of 2020, as a way to get through and document the COVID pandemic. Led by her colleague, Bri Webber, we journaled for at least two more years, our numbers dwindling, as they always do. Bri and Analyn Revilla hung on, then had to respond to other demands. Phoenix Smith and Bennie Thomas and I are still getting together via Zoom more Mondays than not.

While I am grateful for the inspiration, I'm even more grateful for the friendship these women have shown me.

To Phoenix and Bennie

January 2-3, 1989

The case started with the room. Or, rather, Sid and I got sucked into the case because of what happened in the room in September 1952.

But Sid and I didn't know that when Jay Fedders first left a message on our home answering machine a couple days before New Year's. Since Fedders said he was an editor for a newsweekly, and since Sid and I work as freelance writers, we eventually returned the call.

Sid had already verified that Fedders worked on the magazine he said he did. It may seem a little paranoid. Our problem is that freelance writing is only the visible part of our lives (and I wasn't doing that much of it at that time, anyway). The hidden part is that we are undercover operatives for a government agency so secret only its members and a few liaisons know it exists. Which is why we get cautious when someone calls us out of the blue. On the other hand, editors sometimes do, and neither Sid nor I like turning down writing work.

So when Fedders checked out and Sid called back and Fedders found out we were actually in New York at the time, we agreed to go to lunch. We met Fedders at a deli in Midtown Manhattan, on the ground floor of the building where he worked. He was a medium-sized man, probably in his early forties. His half-glasses sat on top of thinning blond hair, the chain hanging down his back.

"It's good to meet you two," Fedders said after we ordered. "My colleague at World of Real Estate has a lot of good things to say about you. Especially you, Sid."

"Well, Mike's a good guy to work for," Sid said with a smile.

I smiled, too. Mike had darned well better be saying good things about Sid and me. He usually called because something had gone wrong and he needed a story yesterday. We had pulled his fat out of the fire so many times, we put on fireproof gloves when he called. [But he was still one of the nicer guys we wrote for. – SEH]

"And he's a real pain in the backside," Fedders said, laughing.

I darned near bit my tongue in half. We waited as the waitress brought me a huge pastrami sandwich on rye with potato salad on the side, a nice bit of chicken salad for Sid and a Reuben for Fedders.

"But I didn't call you to bash Mike, as entertaining as that can be," Fedders continued with a laugh. "There's something else I want to talk to you about. I was figuring I could catch up with you, Sid, right after the Consumer Electronics Show later this month. I'll be heading to Northern California to follow some stuff up and figured we could meet then. But this is even better. So what brings you to the big city?"

Sid smiled. "Holidays with the family."

"You still got relatives here?"

"One, and not for long. It's a long story." Sid nibbled a bit of chicken salad. "So why are you looking to meet with us?"

Fedders chortled. "It's not related to a writing job. Sorry about that, but there it is. However, I think this will be of interest to you. My wife, Petra, and I bought this brownstone not far from the financial district about three years ago. We've been restoring it. So a few months ago, we take apart this one room and find this ledger with half of it in code, and half of it with what looks like real names." Fedders grinned. "Including one Sheila Hackbirn."

"I see," said Sid.

I could see Sid forcing himself to keep his face blank. It wasn't terribly surprising. Sid's last name is Hackbirn. He finally nodded politely, but clearly didn't want to share more until he knew what Fedders wanted.

"Here's what gets interesting," Fedders continued, oblivious to Sid's reaction. "We've found out that the place was a whorehouse for a lot of rich and powerful men, and that one of the girls, a Sheila Hackbirn, was found dead in her room there. Murdered, and it was never solved."

"So I've heard." Sid's smile was stiff, polite, and just sad enough.

"You knew her?"

"Of her," Sid replied.

He was acting indifferent, which was not a good sign. I totally got why he was being so cagey. We're alive because we don't take that kind of chance, and we didn't know Fedders from Adam. But there was something else going on, too.

"Huh." Fedders took a big bite of his sandwich, then spoke as he chewed. "The police reports that I looked up? They mention a sister of the victim. A Stella Caponetti. You know her?"

"My aunt." Sid cleared his throat. "Sheila Hackbirn was my mother. I was only two when she died, so I never knew her."

"No kidding!" Fedders all but bounced out of his seat. "That's awesome. That settles it. You gotta come by. We think we figured out which room it happened in."

"Uh..." Sid smiled stiffly again. "Thanks, but no thanks."

"But maybe we can figure out who killed her."

Sid glanced at me. "That would be nice but seems pretty unlikely at this point. I appreciate the offer, Jay. I really do. But it's not just about me. There's my aunt to consider. She's the one who raised me. Somehow, I think this would rake up more pain than necessary, if you know what I mean."

"Oh. Uh. Yeah." Fedders looked a touch chagrined. "I suppose it might. Well, talk to her about it. You never know."

"True." Sid focused on his chicken salad.

The conversation meandered elsewhere, although Fedders gently hinted multiple times that it would be great if Sid and Stella saw the room. Sid and I finished lunch, leaving Fedders hanging.

"So why didn't you want to see the room?" I asked Sid as we walked uptown to the apartment belonging to Stella's lover, Sy Flournoy.

Sid gazed over at the traffic on Park Avenue. He's not a tall man, just barely three inches taller than me, and I'm average. He has dark, wavy hair, bright blue eyes, and a dimpled chin.

"Stella." He smiled at me. "You know how she is about her sister. She told me hardly anything about Sheila when

I was a kid, and still won't say much. And when she does, she totally shuts down."

"Still, we could have looked at it ourselves. Aren't you even the least bit curious?"

"Yeah, but I didn't want Fedders to know that. Which is why I said no." He shrugged. "And I am concerned about how Stella would react."

I made a face. "Yeah. That makes sense. At the same time, it seems kind of unfair to not tell her about Fedders."

"I know. Let's see what kind of mood Stella's in when we get back to the apartment. Like Fedders said, you never know."

The Whole Fam-Damily was at the apartment when we got back, lounging or reading. Fam-Damily was a joke my nephew Darby had made the year before and thought he was really getting away with something. Only it seems to have stuck. The family consists of my parents, Bill and Althea Wycherly, Sy and Stella (who are functionally Sid's parents), my sister Mae and her husband, Neil O'Malley, their six kids (Darby, Janey, Ellen, Mitch, Marty, and Lissy), Sid, me, and our son, Nick, who was 15, almost 16.

The reason we had celebrated Christmas at Sy's apartment was that it would be the last time we'd have a chance to. Sy was retiring as head of the strings department at Juilliard and moving to the Los Angeles area, where all the rest of us lived, except my parents. As in, Sy and Stella were finally going to be living together, something they hadn't done since they were undergraduates back in the 1940s. Yeah, that was one of those things that I had to respect but would have rather barged in and asked.

Sy's apartment was mostly empty except for our things and some rented furniture. He and Stella had cleared out everything the week before we'd arrived, so that Sy could rent it out. It was surprisingly large for a New York city apartment. The rooms were laid out in a long line, with the kitchen and utility room at one end, the dining room, living room, the study, then four bedrooms, each with its own bathroom.

Sy's family had owned the place since the building was built in the late 'thirties. Or maybe it was older than that. The exterior of the building certainly had the clean lines of that time.

"Did you two have a nice lunch out?" Mama asked when we got back. She's small and birdlike, with a will of iron.

"Nice enough," said Sid, pulling off his topcoat.

I took the coat and went to put it in our bedroom. When I got back to the bedroom, Stella was cursing at Sid.

"Why on earth would you think that?" she snarled. Stella is short, although taller than Mama. Her hair is dark gray, wavy like Sid's, and she has Sid's blue eyes and cleft chin. "It's the not knowing what happened to her that's so hard to take."

"Well, excuse me if I can't read your mind." Sid paced in the living room that seemed oddly vacant of family members except for Sy and me.

Sy's a tall man, with balding white hair and beard, and a full belly. He watched Sid and Stella with a resigned look on his face. Not that there was anything unusual about Sid and Stella fighting with each other. They mostly got along, but it had never been an easy relationship.

Stella snorted. "I would think you would understand."

"Understand what?" Sid snapped. "You almost never talk about her, and the few times you do, it's with complete disdain! I haven't got anything to go on here except your anger."

"My dear," Sy interrupted, his voice ponderous. Ponderous was his usual mode of speech, but it got exceptionally so when he was dealing with Stella in one of her more difficult moods. "Perhaps we should simply ask Sid if he would be so good as to contact this Fedders person and ask to see the room after all."

Sid blew his breath out. "I can do that."

He watched Stella, his eyes blazing as brilliantly as hers.

She sniffed, then pulled herself up even straighter. "Then do it."

Sid called Jay Fedders and arranged to meet him in the middle of the afternoon the next day. Mae and Mama took care of ordering dinner for that night and getting it delivered.

One of the challenges we face as a group when we're traveling is the wide diversity of ages among the kids. Lissy was only two and a half that January and Nick and Darby were both almost 16. It's one we embrace, and in this case, meant that several evenings were spent in the apartment. That night, Mama and Daddy took the youngest kids out to a movie. The rest of us sprawled around the apartment reading.

The next day, we all spent the morning at the Central Park Zoo. But then Sid, Sy, Stella, and I had to head downtown to meet Fedders at his brownstone.

It looked pretty typical for the area, with several steps up the stoop to the front door and a rough gray brick exterior.

Fedders' wife was gone. He was all smiles as he let the four of us in, then ushered us upstairs.

"Well, here it is. The room where it happened."

Fedders opened the door to the room. I stepped back from the doorway to let Sid and Stella enter the room first. Once inside, Sid put his arm around Stella's shoulder, but she didn't seem to notice. Sy rested his hand on my shoulder and gave it a squeeze. This would not be easy for him, either.

Sid can keep a pretty tight leash on his emotions, something that used to make me crazy when we first knew each other. And though he's gotten a lot better at talking to me about his feelings, I couldn't read him at that moment. There was something going on, but I didn't know what.

Stella, for her part, seemed even more shut down than usual as she looked around the room with the tulip wallpaper and dark colonial-style bedroom furniture.

"We're pretty sure this is where it happened." Fedders nodded at the wallpaper. "We were lucky to find that stuff. It matches the wallpaper in the crime scene photos, and as we scraped down the walls in all the rooms, this was the only one that had that pattern."

Stella nodded. "She always liked tulips."

"Huh," Sid replied, his voice flat.

"And here's the ledger," Fedders said, then paused.

Stella nodded and Fedders placed the small ledger on the full-size bed with the pink bedspread. Stella shifted out from under Sid's arm and went to the bed. She touched the small pasteboard binder filled with lined paper covered over in narrow but neat handwriting.

"Any chance we can find out who her johns were?" she asked.

Fedders winced. "If we can find someone to read the code, maybe."

I glanced over at Sid. He's actually pretty good at code breaking and we knew a couple of people who were even better at it. But that was the part of our lives that we can't talk about.

"Wealthy, powerful men," Stella grumbled, her bitterness finally adding some life to her voice.

"My darling," Sy said, his voice subdued, but still sonorous. "Perhaps it is time for us to make our way home."

Stella nodded, then looked over at Sid. "Are you alright?"

"I'm fine," Sid replied a little too quickly. "I'm more worried about you right now."

Stella took a deep breath. "I am well enough." Her bright blue eyes turned on Fedders. "I would like a copy of the ledger."

"Absolutely," Fedders said. "The more people we have looking at this, the better our chances we'll be able to find out what happened here."

"We shall see," Stella said, her voice flat again. "We'll stay in touch."

Fedders smiled, and we agreed.

In the cab on the way back to Sy's apartment on the Upper East Side, Stella insisted that we not tell the rest of the family about Fedders and the brownstone.

"I do not want to be answering any questions until I've had a chance to think this through," she said.

"I suppose that's fair," Sy said.

"Fine," said Sid, letting out his breath. "Any thoughts on what we want for dinner?"

I wasn't exactly thrilled about letting things go, let alone thinking it was a pretty unrealistic request given the argument the day before. But there wasn't much I could do about it. Stella had made up her mind and Sid and Sy both felt they had to honor that.

Sid and Darby took over getting dinner ordered and picked up. Mae and Neil went out for dinner to get some time for themselves. I could tell that Mama wanted to know about that afternoon, but had to respect that Stella didn't want to talk about it.

After dinner arrived and we ate, Sy took the eight-year-old twins, Marty and Mitch, to the apartment's study to give them a lesson in trumpet and French horn. Sy may have focused on strings, but I don't think there's an instrument he can't play, or teach, for that matter. All of Mae's kids, except Lissy, who was only two, play some instrument or another. However, we gravely fear that Marty talked his brother into playing brass to be as annoying as possible. Mama thinks it was more likely that they wanted to avoid competing with Darby, who's a violinist and very talented. Even odds either way.

Stella read in the living room, holding Lissy, who was sleeping in spite of the horn lesson. Ellen, age 10, sat reading next to Stella. Mama lounged in a nearby chair with her book. Daddy got a poker game going for the rest of us at the rented table in the dining room.

Poker remains a very popular family activity, never mind all the complaints that it's almost impossible to beat Daddy, me, or Janey. [We're just humoring you guys. We can beat you. Occasionally. - SEH] I drew the high card for the first deal, and we each took turns around the table calling and dealing games.

We'd gone around the table at least three times. Daddy dealt a hand of five-card draw. I pulled a pair of jacks in the first deal, worth staying in for, but not that exciting, and it didn't look like anyone had pulled anything terribly good. I checked, then Janey, age 13, and Nick did (as in decided whether or not to bet based on who made the first bet). Darby opened the betting with a penny bet. The rest of us called. Daddy asked us how many cards we each wanted for the second deal. I got three cards, Janey took two, Nick three cards, Darby three, Sid got one, and Daddy folded. Sid took one card? Either he was bluffing or hoping he'd fill out something.

As Sid picked up the card that Daddy dealt him, I saw it. The tell. Whatever Sid had gotten, it was pretty damned good. I still had my pair of jacks and had gotten the third in the draw. But I knew that look and the second Daddy called for the first bet, I folded. Even odds Janey had caught the tell - she's really good that way and even better with Sid. She folded promptly. Nick and Darby picked up on it and folded as well.

Sid looked at us, utterly disgusted, and it wasn't the particularly bad trumpet note.

"It's time for me to cash out," he grumbled, throwing his cards onto the table.

I looked at my watch. "You know. I think I'll cash out, too."

It was getting rather late and Sid, being a morning person, means that we're usually in bed by ten or eleven at night. I'm not sure if the others continued playing. But I followed Sid to the back of the apartment and the bedroom we were sleeping in.

"What's going on?" I asked as he pulled off his snowy-white dress shirt.

"Isn't there enough going on?" He glared at me.

"Come on, Sid," I groaned. "Cashing out after a bad hand? That's not your usual style."

"It wasn't a bad hand," he snapped, viciously tossing the shirt onto his suitcase. "It was a nine-high straight flush. How often does that come along?" He sprinkled curse words throughout his rant. "But you had to go and read my mind and lead the folding."

"I can't read minds. Your eyebrow quirked and you got that little grin you get when you're about to get laid. Janey was onto you."

Sid snorted, mostly because he knew I was right. I mean, it's not like I didn't understand how he felt about that hand. It is insanely frustrating to get a really good hand, only to have everyone at the table spot it and fold before you can make any decent cash on it. But there was more.

"It was only for less than a second," I said, trying to be consoling. Then I touched his arm. "What's really going on?"

His sigh slid up from the depths of his being.

"I'm not sure," he said, wincing. "I really didn't think seeing that room today was going to be any big deal. But now..." He blinked and shook his head. "In some ways, it was like the woman who gave birth to me was this vague fictional character. If people wanted to make up for any-thing it was that I didn't have a father. Stella was there, so I was covered on the mother front, I guess. But guys trying to be father figures? Crap. It was like they were trying to save me from some fatal disease or something. They were coming out of the woodwork to be my father." He snorted. "Which is ironic as hell because the guys who were, in fact, doing the job didn't pull that stuff." Okay. He didn't say stuff. Sid's language is usually pretty blue.

"Sy taught me how to pee standing up, which is one of those things that can be a little hard for a woman to teach a boy."

"Huh." My brow creased. "How did Nick learn then? I mean, I'm pretty sure he does."

Nick had been raised by his first mom, the woman who gave birth to him, and her mother until he was ten. That's when his grandmother had died. Then Rachel brought him to us when Nick was a few days short of his eleventh birthday because Rachel had been diagnosed with leukemia. She died when Nick was twelve and I became Nick's second mom and later adopted him.

"He stands." Sid nodded. "He doesn't remember how he learned, though."

We both winced at that. We know very little about Nick's life before he came to us besides what he remembers. Rachel had not been very good at sharing that kind of information.

Sid waved his hand. "That's all irrelevant anyway. The thing is, my birth mother was never very real to me. Stella wouldn't talk about her, and I just accepted it. I had a photograph and that was it." He sank onto the bed and gazed at the floor. "But today... First, Stella gets all freaked out. Then, it was as though Sheila Hackbirn came to life for the first time. Like it finally hit me that she was a real person." He looked up at me. "How do I react to that? Grief? Anger? I have no idea."

"All of the above, none of the above?" I sat down next to him and held him. "I'm pretty confident you'll figure it all out, though."

He squeezed me back. "Not without you, I won't."

He kissed the side of my head, and the two of us slid onto our backs. And things went where they normally go at that time of night.

January 4, 1989

The next morning, Sid hauled me down to the base-ment and the building's fitness center at six-thirty that morning to get a run on the treadmills there. Sid had found it shortly after we arrived while doing some stair climbing to make up for it being too cold and snowy to run outside. Sy had been surprised to find that the building had a fitness center, which was odd, because he'd only been living there since the early '70s when his father passed away. He later inherited the apartment from his mother, who had died a few years later.

Sid showered before I did, and I went to help get break-fast laid out. Sy had called in an order to a local delicatessen the night before, and since no one else was awake at that ungodly hour, twelve-year-old Janey had taken delivery on the huge box of bagels, cream cheese, lox and capers, with some lettuce and tomato slices. It happens that way. Sid and Janey are the only morning people in the family.

I staggered back to our room just as Sid was getting out of the shower. He grinned when he heard about the bagels and lox. Then I got into the shower and tried to wake up.

Dressed in a sweater and jeans, I went into the dining room.

"You two were busier than usual last night," Neil was telling Sid.

"Neil!" Mae shoved her husband with fond irritation.

Sid focused on layering a bagel half with cream cheese, lox, and a tomato slice.

"At least you didn't bang on the wall." I grumbled.

Mae and Neil had the bedroom next to ours, mostly because of the noise issue. Sid and I were trying to keep it down. We just don't always succeed.

Mae, my older sister, is shorter than me and with a rounder figure than mine. But we both have the same brown hair. She grows hers out straight and cuts it short. I like mine longer. Neil, on the other hand, is tall and lanky, with the same red hair that he passed on to Darby, the twins, and Lissy. In fact, we have some photos of Neil when he was sixteen, and he looked almost exactly like Darby does now at age fifteen.

"Yeah, well." Neil's grin was less than innocent as he pushed his glasses up on his nose. "We might have been a little busy ourselves."

"Neil!" Mae gasped even louder and flushed a deep red. Then she giggled.

Sid shook his head. "You two had better be careful. That's how you ended up with Lissy."

"Sid!" Mae snarled. "Will you cut it out?"

Sid pointed at her. "You're the one who keeps blaming her conception on me."

Just to be clear. Sid used to sleep around a lot, and was incredibly popular, too. For good reason, I have to say. But Mae has no actual knowledge of how good. It's just that Neil once asked Sid the secret of Sid's popularity. Sid told him - whatever it was. He's never told me. [A- you never asked me to, and B- you already knew what it was because I'd explained it to you before any number of times, albeit not in those terms. - SEH] Anyway, Mae confessed to me that things had gotten better between her and Neil after that night, which is why she blames Lissy on Sid.

"Not going to happen, Sid." Neil smirked as I flopped into a nearby chair. "We've learned our lesson and taken yet another cue from you."

Sid laughed hard as I gaped.

"You got fixed?" Sid said.

"We weren't going to say anything about that," Mae hissed at her husband, then looked at me. "I'm sorry, Lisa."

I'd had some trouble right before Sid and I got married almost three years before because Sid and I can't have kids together. Sid got a vasectomy back in late 1972 (after he'd conceived Nick, although he didn't know he had). As much sleeping around as he was doing, it was the responsible thing to do, especially since he couldn't have imagined wanting to get married or wanting a child.

I shrugged as I grabbed a bagel. "I'm pretty much over it."

The sound of Mama's voice giving either Darby or Nick what for floated into the dining room.

"Having an adolescent can do that to you," I continued, splitting open the pumpernickel bagel.

"Tell me about it." Mae sighed and got up.

She planted a kiss on Neil's hair, and he patted her backside. She returned a minute later with the news that it wasn't Darby or Nick who'd sassed Grandma, but Marty, who at eight years old hadn't learned the difference between smart aleck and going too far. Come to think of it, Darby and Nick hadn't entirely learned the difference, either. The living room phone rang, and a minute later, Mitch, Marty's identical twin, came running in.

"Uncle Sid, a Mr. Fedders is on the phone for you," Mitch said.

"Thank you." Sid got up and ruffled Mitch's hair. "I'll get it."

I finished piling cream cheese, lettuce, tomato, lox and capers onto the two halves of the pumpernickel bagel and on another two halves of a plain bagel, and started eating.

Stella joined Neil, Mae and me in the dining room a couple of minutes later. She looked pretty bleary-eyed, and I had to wonder how much sleep she'd gotten that night. I debated asking, but with Stella the odds were only even she'd admit that she'd had a bad night.

Stella has a lot of issues with her nuclear family, most of them deserved. Um, let's just say that it wasn't a coincidence that Stella's younger sister turned tricks to make their living. Which is only one of the reasons Stella didn't talk about her family. She was determined to bury that part of her life in the past and, really, you could hardly blame her.

Sy came into the dining room, sat down next to Stella, and whispered in her ear.

"Of course, I'm certain!" she snapped.

Sid appeared in the open doorway between the dining room and the living room, my mother behind him.

"Stella, I'm perfectly happy to look at the photos for you," Sid said. He glanced at me.

"I will look at them," Stella growled. "You do not have to coddle me. I am a grown woman and perfectly capable of handling myself."

"Oh, Stella, honey." Mama sighed. "Nobody is saying you're not. It's just that this can't be easy for you. I mean, I wouldn't want to look at crime scene photos, especially if somebody I knew was in them."

"Crime scene photos?" I looked over at Sid.

"Yeah." Sid nodded and sighed. He had on an off-white Aran Isles sweater over his blue sport shirt and really tight jeans. "Jay Fedders has been in touch with the woman who has the original casebook. Or access to it. She's a detective with the N.Y.P.D., and her father was the detective on the case originally. Fedders called her yesterday after we left, and she's agreed to let us look at the photos and the reports. The photos are pretty grim, she said."

"I want to find out who killed my sister," Stella said, her eyes blazing. "God knows, no one gave a damn at the time!"

Mama winced. She hates foul language and damn counts. But I guess she figured that if anyone had a right to curse at that moment, Stella did.

"Well, we clearly care now." Sid's voice got on the acerbic side. He sighed, then glanced at me again. "I've got an appointment for one o'clock at Detective Reilly's precinct station."

Sy cleared his throat. "Then I say it is time we followed Lisa's excellent example and apply ourselves to our morning repast."

"We'll still be able to spend some time at the World Trade Center before we go," Stella said, helping herself to an onion bagel.

Sid finished his bagel quickly. He and Mae started cleaning up before everybody was done, but as soon as I'd finished, Sid pulled me aside and we went to our bedroom.

"You don't have to go if you don't want to," he told me.

"I know." I smiled at him, then took a deep breath. "But I think I'd better."

"I can handle—"

"I know you can. It's for me." I swallowed. "Desensitization. Remember?"

Sid nodded and held me. I have this phobia of corpses, which can be a real problem in Sid's and my work for the organization within the FBI known as Operation Quickline. It's primarily a courier group, but we also do some investigative work. Quickline is how I got my phobia. The one good thing about it is that no one is going to suspect me of being an operative when they see me barfing over a stiff. And I'd been working on the problem with a really good trauma shrink for several years by that point. So it was getting better. Which was why I wanted to look at the photos.

We all made it out and headed downtown on the subway. We ate lunch on Mott Street, then Sy, Stella, Sid, and I headed to our appointment.

I was surprised that Detective Jane Reilly worked in a fairly modern building. The detectives' room was an open space filled with ugly metal desks, most of them piled high with binders and other papers. Reilly was tall, with dark curly hair, pulled back into a ponytail at the nape of her neck. She wore a navy polyester suit jacket over a shiny blue blouse, and matching navy pants.

"Good to meet you folks," she said, shaking each of our hands. Her eyes lingered briefly on Stella, then Sid, and she got a tiny glint in her eyes as she noted the family resemblance. "I appreciate you guys coming in. Come on. I've got the casebook in the conference room."

"How did you get involved on the case?" Sid asked her as we walked down a nearby hallway.

"I'm not officially," Reilly said. "It was my dad's case. I don't know if you'd understand, but sometimes a case just sticks with you. This one was Dad's. He told me that it went cold almost immediately. Then someone higher up ordered him to let it go."

"Wealthy, powerful men," Stella whispered.

"I'm afraid so," Reilly said. She paused in front of a door. "It really pissed Dad off. He always said that the vic had a sister. She had a child. How could they just let her go?" She shuddered briefly. "Anyway, the pictures are not pretty."

Sid held Stella's shoulders as the two went over to the table where the black and white prints were laid out. Sy stepped up and put his hand on Stella's back. I swallowed the twisting in my gut and went to look, too.

There were dark stains all over the bed, and the body lay crumpled under the dark bedside table. The table, which looked black in the photo, was fairly shallow, with four small drawers on the top half, and a larger one below. The whole thing stood on four squat pillars, and the top had sharp, protruding corners.

"They said her head was bashed in," Stella said, her voice going even flatter than it had the day before.

"Possibly on the corner of that nightstand," said Sid.

"Hm." It was hard to tell if Stella agreed with him or not.

Reilly pointed to the front left corner of the nightstand. "They found some hairs and blood there. The blood type matched the, uh, victim."

Stella nodded once more. "Is there a way to get a copy of these?"

"I shouldn't." Reilly sighed. "It is totally against policy. But you know what? I'll find a way to get a copy of the whole casebook to you."

She led us from the room, and we followed her back through the open detectives room downstairs toward the front door of the precinct house.

"Dad kind of passed the case onto me," Reilly continued as we walked. "I was so glad when Jay started bugging me about it. It gave me an excuse to look at it again."

Stella paused on the stair, her brow creased. "So someone did care."

"My dad," Reilly said, her voice small and sad. "Yeah. He cared a lot."

"Cared?" Sid asked, gently.

"Yeah. He, uh, passed away a couple years ago." Reilly gave us a pained smile.

"I'm so sorry," Stella said even before I could.

Her voice was soft and tender, too. Not her usual tone by any stretch. But one thing I have come to appreciate about Stella is that the second you think you've got her pegged, you discover you haven't. Not unlike Sid, now that I think about it.

"Thanks," Reilly said with a shrug. "He lived a good, long life and died in bed from a heart attack. He's the reason I became a cop. So was this case, in a way. Mom had just told Dad that she was pregnant with me when it went down. Dad would take me to the station to look at the case book to hide that he was still trying to find the killer. He had to be careful how he did it because with my four older brothers and me to support, he couldn't afford to get into trouble."

We arrived at the glass door to the building.

"I can't thank you enough, Detective," Stella said, offering her right hand.

"I haven't done anything," Reilly said. "At least, not yet. But Jay's right. The more people we have looking at this, the better the odds we'll find out something. Heck, you might think of something that didn't occur to you at the time. And fortunately, plenty of the people involved are still alive."

"Well, we appreciate all you're doing," Sid said, then gave Reilly our business card. "You can send whatever you can to this address. I'll pay for the shipping, too."

"Thank you," Reilly said.

We all shook hands again, then Sy, Sid, Stella and I left.

January 6–7, 1989

As I've already noted, Sid and I are not thrilled when people we don't know try to get a hold of us. But we do need a cover career to hide behind, and being freelance writers is a darned handy one when we're asking nosy questions that we otherwise couldn't. So Sid has business cards with our rented mailbox address on it. We've set it up so that our house address is not linked to any of our phone numbers.

And people being who they are, they sometimes hand out our address and phone number without checking with us first. We can't complain too much because we get some of our writing work that way. And it was how Jay Fedders got a hold of us. The other editor had just given him our phone number. Then Fedders passed it on to someone else.

At least, that's what Congressman James Van Blinn said in the message he left on our answering machine. Fedders had heard about Van Blinn from Detective Reilly. Reilly, for her part, called to let us know that she had not told Van Blinn anything about us, but had put him onto Fedders.

"I didn't want to say anything in front of your aunt," Reilly said when Sid called her back. "But Dad thought that Van Blinn may have been one of those wealthy powerful men behind the case getting let go. Van Blinn seems on the level, but he's been sniffing around ever since the murder happened."

Sid had put her on the speakerphone in the office.

"Well, that's interesting," Sid said, his eyebrow quirking.

"It is," Reilly said. "I put Fedders onto him in the hopes that he'd be able to lean on the old fart in a way that I can't. Sorry about Fedders giving him your information. I swear this will be the last time I trust him with anything like that."

"That's alright." Sid chuckled a little. "It happens all the time. We don't like it, but it does."

"On the other hand, would you mind talking to Van Blinn?" Reilly asked. "That whole leaning on him thing."

Sid sighed and looked over at me. I nodded.

"I'll see what I can do. Thanks for calling."

He shook his head as he pressed the off switch on the phone.

Sid, Nick, and I had flown home on Thursday, the day after we had gone to the precinct house to meet with Reilly. Sid and I had figured that there would be a rush of work (both visible and not) to handle the following Monday after the holiday break, and wanted to take a day to prep before spending that weekend helping to clear Stella's condo enough to make room for whatever Sy had decided to keep from his family's place.

Which is why, that Friday morning, Sid and I were in our office listening to answering machine messages and calling people back. Nick was in his room or in the library, either reading or talking to his friend Josh on the phone.

"You okay?" I asked Sid.

Our desks are butted up against the other, so that Sid and I face each other when we work. Long John Silver, our gray cat with one eye, sat snuggled in Sid's lap as usual. Motley, our springer spaniel with liver-colored spots, lay next to my desk, snoozing away, as he usually did. Fritz and Blueberry, Long John's offspring, were elsewhere, probably outside in Fritz's case. Blueberry preferred crashing in the living room, usually on a shelf. Bowser, the puppy, was running around the backyard.

Sid made a face. "I don't know. I think I'm okay. I mean, I am curious. Even if Sheila wasn't that real to me, it is a part of my history, and it would be interesting to know what happened. But then there's Stella's anger about it. Yeah, it's justified, but I don't know that I want to hook into it." He blinked and shook his head as if trying to clear it. "I've spent too much time being angry."

I nodded. Sid's a Vietnam veteran, and when he got drafted and chose to go into the Army, it estranged him from Stella. It was his anger when he got home that continued the estrangement until late 1985.

"The problem is," Sid continued, and winced. "We are pretty damn good at investigating things. So would it be an abuse of our privilege to check things out?"

I looked at him. "You're not usually that worried about taking advantage of our jobs."

"You're right." Sid's face creased even harder. "That's another thing that's bothering me. Maybe I don't want to know what happened. Maybe it's better buried in the past. It doesn't really change anything or affect me."

"True." I looked over the bit of work I was trying to get done. "But it affects Stella, and she does not seem to be dealing all that well with this."

Sid's breath released with a whoosh. "Which is the crux of the issue. This isn't about my history. It's about hers and how she's able to deal with it. And there's only so much we can do about it."

"But if we can help her along..."

"There's that, too." Sid rolled his eyes.

I reached across my desk and grabbed his hand. "There's no reason you have to answer Van Blinn's message now. Why don't we give it a few days?"

Sid agreed, and we went back to work. Sid got the freelancing work organized, while I went over my syllabus for the two sections of Basic Composition that I'd be teaching when school started the following week. Then I updated the notes and outlines for my two independent studies projects for my Monday meetings with each of the two professors supervising the projects, plus got in some advance reading on the one lecture class I was taking that semester.

The summer after Sid and I had gotten married, he talked me into following one of my big dreams, that of getting my PhD in English. This semester was the last of my coursework before I really knuckled down on my dissertation. It looked like it was going to be a fascinating semester, class-wise, but a busy one.

As for Congressman Van Blinn, well, he didn't get to where he was by not being tenacious. Sid had the misfortune to pick up when the congressman called. Since Sid was working on an outline at the time, he slapped the speaker phone on so that he could keep writing as he talked.

"Hello?" Sid asked.

We don't identify ourselves until we know who's on the other end of the line.

"Eh. This is Congressman James Van Blinn," said the soft, comfortable tenor through the phone's speaker. "I'm trying to reach a Mr. Sid Hackbirn."

Sid glanced my way. I shrugged and nodded.

"This is he," Sid said.

"Ah. Good. I hope you got my earlier message."

"I did."

"Then you know that Mr. Fedders referred me to you regarding the murder of..." Van Blinn seemed to swallow. "Well, eh."

"And what's your interest in the case?" Sid asked, a little curtly. But then again, he clearly wasn't sure what he was dealing with and wasn't about to give away anything until he knew.

"I, eh, knew Sheila Hackbirn. We were very close."

"I'm sure you were."

"No! No. It wasn't like that, son."

I could see Sid bristling and held up my hand.

"I see," Sid said to the speakerphone.

Van Blinn chuckled. "I doubt that."

Sid and I both rolled our eyes.

"But," Van Blinn continued quickly. "Of course, you couldn't possibly have known. You were just a baby then. The way her case was handled, well, it was a terrible injustice. I've been trying to fix it ever since. I mean that. That's why I want to talk to you. To tell you about her. Maybe then we can find the man who killed her."

Sid sighed. "Alright. But I'm not in New York right now."

"I know. Well, I know you live in Los Angeles. I'm in Orange County right now, myself. Visiting with an old friend from that time. In fact, Earline may be able to shed some light on this, as well." Van Blinn coughed lightly. "I'd like to invite you to lunch this coming week. There's a lovely old club, the Los Angeles Country Club."

"I'm familiar with it," Sid said.

"Would Tuesday be good for you?"

Sid glanced at me and shook his head. "Can you hold on for a second?"

"Sure."

Sid put the congressman on hold. "Do you want to come?"

I frowned. "Do you want me there?"

"I asked you first."

My eyes rolled. "I can be if you want me there. It's first day of classes, though, so it might be tight. I've got a break between my lecture class and my first section of Basic Comp. And the college isn't that far from mid-Wilshire."

"I can probably push it to Wednesday, too." Sid frowned as he thought. "Let's see what Van Blinn wants to do."

He pushed the buttons for the speakerphone again.

"Congressman? We can meet, but Wednesday would be better for my wife and me. And Stella."

"Eh." Van Blinn coughed, then chuckled. "Well, son, that would be a problem. I was hoping to meet you by yourself, and I'm afraid Wednesday would not be a good day for me."

Sid shook his head. "I'm afraid that is a problem for me. Tell you what. I'll see what I can do on my end, perhaps for later in the week. Is there a number where I can reach you?"

Van Blinn rattled off a number with an Orange County area code, then added his New York office so that Sid could leave a message, if necessary.

"I hope you reconsider, son," Van Blinn said. "I understand why you're... being cautious. But I believe this will be good for you."

"We shall see. Good afternoon." Sid hung up and shook his head.

I raised my eyebrows. "Sounds like a power-over game to me."

"Possibly. Probably." Sid got up and started pacing. "And you know what? I am not in the mood to play. Damn it, I am not his son, and I do not need to be jerked around by someone with paternal fantasies. Especially when it's as possible as not that he was the one who killed Sheila, and is only sticking his nose in now so that he can keep us off the scent."

"Okay. Do you want to mention him to Stella?"

"We'll see."

And we each went back to our respective work.

It was a good thing that we'd gotten that extra day at home before Stella and Sy arrived from New York. Their plane arrived at seven that evening. Sid and I picked them up and drove them to the condo on Wilshire. We'd driven Nick and his best friend Josh Sandoval to the mall around five. Josh's father, Reuben, got the boys right before the mall closed and brought Nick home close to nine-thirty. Sid and I sent Nick to bed shortly after that. We needed to be at Stella's fairly early and were figuring the next day was going to be pretty stressful.

It most certainly was. Stella snapped at everyone, especially Sid. Even Sy, who is normally quite easy going, got a little waspish as he tried, unsuccessfully, to get Stella to back down a little. Finally, late that afternoon, Stella kicked Sid, Nick, and me out, and we were happy to go.

"What is going on with Stella?" Nick complained as we drove back to our house in Beverly Hills.

Even Nick had gotten snarled at, and given how indulgent Stella usually is with him, it completely shocked the boy. He's got the same blue eyes, dark wavy hair, and cleft chin that Sid and Stella have, but he was almost six feet tall, and had wisps of a dark beard on his cheeks and chin.

"I don't know," Sid said with a deep sigh.

I was driving because Sid was in no shape to, being exhausted from trying not to respond to Stella's sniping.

"I don't think it's Sy moving in," I said.

"I don't either," said Sid. "It's probably her sister's murder."

"That makes sense," said Nick. "I heard Sy whispering something to her, and I think that's what it was about."

Sid shook his head. "Which means we're not going to find out for sure."

"I wonder if Van Blinn got a hold of her." I made a face.

"Who knows?" Sid blinked and shuddered. "But like I said, she's not going to tell us. So I propose we let it all go and focus instead on demolishing a frutti di mare plate and some pasta from our favorite place."

"Yeah!" Nick yelled.

"Sure," I said.

"Dad," Nick asked. "Are you doing okay?"

Sid smiled softly. "Okay enough, son." Sid's brow suddenly creased. "Do you mind me calling you son?"

"I don't care." Nick flopped back in his seat. "It's not like you can call me by name when we're out in public."

It's one of those things we just don't do because of our little side business. There is the very slim possibility someone might latch onto our real names and take advantage of it. But it's mostly about being undercover. If we're already in the habit of not using our names in public, then the odds we'll accidentally use our real names instead of our cover names are drastically lowered.

"Besides," Nick continued. "I am your son. So why not?"

"No reason," said Sid.

I did not believe that, and Sid knew it, which I could see from the way he glanced at me.

We had a lovely dinner, some nice wine and watched a movie on the VCR at home. While Sid seemed more relaxed, I was not so happy about him trying to let it all go.

"Look," I said as Sid and I were getting ready for bed. "I understand that there's not much we can do about Stella not wanting to talk about it. But we also know that's how things get really messed up."

"Yeah, it is." Sid tossed his sport shirt into the hamper with more force than necessary. "But what are our options here? I can't exactly stick a gun in her face and tell her to talk or else."

"As if that tactic has ever worked." I glared at my toothbrush.

"It's not that." Sid sighed again. "It's just that if Stella doesn't want to talk about it, she's not going to. She's been getting better about it, but after today, I really do not want to push it."

"Is it because you don't really want to know what happened to your mother?"

Sid sank onto the bench in our closet. "The funny thing is, I think I really do want to know. I'm sorry that I can't seem to make up my mind on that score." He frowned as he tried to parse out his feelings. "You know what it is? It's Stella. I'm curious, but I think I'm pulling back because of her. I've never seen her like this before. She's gotten so flat, and you know she is really upset. It's as though all this hurt and anger is bubbling up in her, and I'm not sure where it's coming from. I understand that she's very bitter about how the case was handled. But how does that square with her feelings about her sister? She hated her sister."

I finished rinsing my mouth and spat. "I don't think Stella hated Sheila." Grabbing a towel, I wiped off my face. "They weren't friends. I remember Stella being very clear about that. My guess is that she had a lot of very mixed feelings about her sister. And then kept a lid on it all to protect you."

Sid snorted. "I guess I should be grateful that she was that worried about hurting me. Still..." He shut his eyes, then pulled himself up from the bench. "I just don't get what good it did. I found out anyway."

He slid his arm around my shoulders and we made our way to our bed.

"I know," I said. "It doesn't always make sense to me, either."

"It's not like I don't understand the need to keep a secret or two." Sid pulled back the covers on his side of the bed. "That's how you and I stay alive, for crying out loud. But this isn't national security here. It's simply a part of my ancestry. I know Stella didn't want that for me, but honestly. How would knowing my mother was a hooker make me run out and do the same?"

"It wouldn't, Sid." I slid under the covers on my side of the bed. "But maybe Stella didn't want you feeling the same sort of shame that she possibly did."

"We knew a few hookers and she wasn't embarrassed or ashamed that we did." Sid got into bed, then scooted over to snuggle next to me. "But she never said word one about not wanting me to hustle." He frowned as he considered something. "No. Remember when she first told us about Sheila being a hooker? I asked Stella why she didn't tell me sooner, and that's when she said she didn't want that for me. As if knowing that my mother was a prostitute was going to somehow magically turn me into one."

"Hm." I thought that over. "You know what that reminds me of? There was this big fundamentalist Christian seminar that I got roped into going to my first year of college. I remember going along with some of it. The guy giving it definitely had some scary issues with women and questioning authority. But one thing he said that almost made sense was that if you want someone to identify counterfeit money, you don't give him a bunch of counterfeits to look at. You give him the real stuff, so that if something doesn't match, he knows to question it."

"That's horse manure," Sid snorted. "What if the currency changes?"

"Christianity is not supposed to change." I rolled my eyes. "But that's beside the point. It's the rationale behind banning books. If you give kids only quote, unquote, good stuff to read, they'll be able to tell when something isn't good."

"Which is also horse manure."

"I know, Sid. But maybe that kind of thinking was behind Stella not telling you anything. If she could erase her past, then maybe you wouldn't be affected by it. It doesn't matter that it didn't work. In fact, that it didn't might be driving some of her fear and anger even now."

"It might at that." Sid sighed deeply. "Maybe knowing what's behind the angst will help dealing with it." He looked over at me. "Odds I can talk you into giving me a back rub?"

I reached over and kissed his forehead. "No odds. That one is a dead cert."

January 9 - 10, 1989

No matter how rocky things had been on Saturday, Stella proved to be contrite on Sunday, and Sy took all five of us out to dinner that night. Things were still on the tense side, but it was not a bad evening at all.

The next morning, while I was in the middle of my first meeting of the day, with the professor for my project to develop baseline standards in English Literature for high school students, I felt my pager vibrate. I had to wait until the meeting was done, but by that time there had been a second page.

The first page was from Lillian Ward, also known as the Dragon, and she was the head of Quickline and one of our supervisors. The second was from Sid with the code for important, but not life or death. Fortunately, I did not have to go all the way to the parking lot to my car and the car phone I had in it. There was a pay phone next to the women's room closest to the English Department offices. I called Sid first, guessing that Lillian had paged us both, and that he'd already called her back.

"Hey, Lover," I said when he picked up.

"Hey, sweetheart. Did you see the page from Lillian?"

"I did. So what's up?"

"We've got a meeting tonight with her and Henry." He paused. "It sounds like a job."

"It does. Well, that's our business."

"Not good timing, though."

"When is it ever?" I closed my eyes, thinking. "What time are we talking about?"

"Lillian wants a dinner meeting," Sid said.

"Why am I thinking that this does not bode well?"

"Because it probably doesn't." Sid chuckled. "So what time does Nick get home?"

"When I get him there," I said. "I'm getting the boys this afternoon."

Which meant picking up Nick, Darby, and their best friend Josh at their high school, dropping Darby off at Stella's music school for his violin lesson, then getting Josh home and Nick, well, he went wherever. Lety Sandoval, Josh's mother, usually picked the boys up in the afternoons, since Sid's and my schedules were filled two days a week with the classes we were both teaching. Sid or I drove in the mornings.

"Oh." I could almost hear Sid biting his tongue. "Where's Lety this afternoon?"

"Kyle broke his tooth over the holidays," I said. Justin and Kyle are Josh's younger brothers. "They did an emergency fix, but he needs to get a more permanent one as soon as possible, and so Lety has to take him to the dentist because Reuben is up to his backside in patients who hurt themselves over the holidays."

Reuben, Lety's husband, is an orthopedic surgeon.

"Neil's going to pick up Darby from violin since Darby has a doctor's appointment in the morning, and Mae will take care of getting him to school," I continued.

"Troop maneuvers," Sid sighed. He is frequently bemused by how complicated our lives get.

I felt for him. "It's our lives, darling."

And it was. Sid and I were getting to the point where we were almost looking forward to Nick getting his driver's license that February when he turned 16. Almost.

When I got back to the house with Nick, I sent him off to do his homework, then went to the office.

"Well?" I asked Sid.

He shrugged. "We've got a meeting at six. Conchetta is not entirely annoyed and will have Nick's dinner out for him."

Conchetta is our housekeeper and can get prickly.

"Okay." I sighed. "What time do we need to leave?"

"About five-thirty."

Which meant we were relatively close to the meeting spot. That was a good thing. Sid had also steered Lillian away from any of the singles hot spots that he used to frequent back when he was sleeping around. Henry was disappointed.

"I thought you weren't worried about Sid's old girlfriends," Henry said as we settled in at the table of a rather nice Mexican place on Santa Monica Boulevard.

He's a tall man with a really, really red face.

I glared at him. "You know darned well I'm not."

Which Henry does because I'm good friends with Henry's former secretary, Angelique Carter, who was also one of Sid's more frequent lovers.

"I don't think we need to perseverate on Sid's past alliances," Lillian said.

She's tall and matronly, and a bit of a prude. Suddenly I got who was the real target of Henry's teasing.

The waiter arrived to take our orders and we continued chit-chatting until our food arrived. We had barely started eating when Lillian shifted and cleared her throat.

"As much as I hate to ruin our appetites, we do have a job to discuss," she said. She looked directly at Sid. "You're not going to like this one. It's basically a surveillance job. We had to tap you for it because the subject recently contacted you about the murder of Sheila Hackbirn."

"Oh," said Sid. He took a deep breath. "So who are we talking about? Jay Fedders or James Van Blinn?"

"Congressman Van Blinn," Lillian said after a quick glance at Henry.

Henry shifted. "Someone at the top of the chain is wondering if the congressman is selling us out to somebody. Well, that's what they're saying."

"Really?" I made a face. "He didn't strike me that way."

"Me neither," Sid said, then groaned. "Crap! Are we talking about a political witch hunt?"

Henry and Lillian looked at each other.

"I thought we were not supposed to get involved in politics," I said.

"We are absolutely not supposed to," Lillian said. "Sadly, that doesn't stop them."

Henry shifted. "The problem is that when these guys get to the top of the heap, they start feeling like they have the right to use our intelligence assets any old way they please. And because they are at the top of the heap, it's almost impossible to tell them no."

"Nor does it seem to matter which side of the aisle you come from," Lillian continued. "We tell them that it's utterly unethical. We keep reminding them that it seriously compromises our credibility as an agency. Nothing gets through. Someone in the Oval or close to it has some axe to grind or wants to get rid of an enemy and he tries to use us to set it up."

"They're called nuisance jobs," Henry said. "And they're usually handled at the floater level so that we can keep as tight a rein on this kind of nonsense as possible."

"Dale O'Connor hates them because the ethics are so rank," Lillian said.

Sid and I aren't sure what Dale's actual title or position is, but he's the top boss, short of the President. [Well, not quite the top boss, as I found out when they finally twisted my arm hard enough to get me to take that miserable job. -SEH] Dale is not one of our favorite people by a long shot, but we have to respect him. However much of a royal pain in the butt he is, he is darned good at what he does, and he does have our country's best interests at heart.

"Steve and Ray started the job last month," Henry said. Steve and Ray are the floater team for the Green Line. "They get most of them since being in New York means they're closer to DC. But they heard Van Blinn trying to get a hold of you, and that the congressman was going to be out here on the West Coast for a while."

"Any hint that Van Blinn is actually selling out to anybody?" Sid asked.

Both Lillian and Henry shook their heads.

"None," Lillian snapped. "But it has gotten about that Van Blinn has been looking into the connection between several senators and some of the savings and loans that have been going under lately."

"The reason for the witch hunt," I grumbled.

"'Fraid so," Henry said. He looked at Sid. "The reason he wants to talk to you about this Sheila Hackbirn. She related to you?"

"Uh, yeah." Sid shifted. "My birth mother. You didn't know?"

Henry shrugged. "You were already cleared several times over by the time you joined my team, so I didn't get much background on you."

"Apparently, Dale didn't think we had that much need to know," Lillian said with a shrug. "Part of that paternal thing he has about you."

All four of us rolled our eyes over that one.

"Let's just hope he keeps his distance from us," I said. "After last summer's blow-up, I'm still working on forgiving him."

Just because I respect the guy does not mean I don't get mad at him. Sid chuckled, even though he was equally angry with Dale and the paternal thing and the events of that previous summer.

Lillian sighed. "I don't doubt. But let's stay focused on Van Blinn. If he does start sniffing around any S&L executives, then we should probably know. But I'm really not that interested unless there is completely hard proof that he's doing something illegal. Our primary concern is national security. Henry and I will massage the report for the higher ups."

(Sid's Voice)

There are so many reasons why I am crazy in love with my sweet Lisa. She's intelligent, passionate, and with an amazing balance between firm values and the ability to bend when appropriate. Though what saved me those first weeks of January, '89, was her compassion. I felt horrible whiplashing back and forth between wanting to know what had happened to my birth mother and wanting to stay as far away from it as possible. But Lisa held steady, supporting my feelings no matter which direction they took.

Then Van Blinn had to stick his nose in. Then we got stuck with the very real nuisance of investigating him for no good reason, which frosted both Lisa and me to our cores.

Poor Lisa felt especially cranky about the job. She is easily the most forgiving person I know, but hypocrisy and abuse of power set her off like nothing else.

No matter our reputation for insubordination, there was only so much Lisa and I could do about the situation. In order to keep the abuses in check, we needed to keep our jobs. So when those kinds of orders came down, we had to at least make like we were obeying them, which usually meant a slog through the bullshit pool. That winter, we were swimming in the deep end.

Neither of us was in a particularly good mood that Tuesday morning when I called Van Blinn. Lety got Nick to school that morning to make up for the day before, so we didn't have to think about that, at least. I'd pick Darby up from All-City Orchestra practice after I'd finished teaching at Stella's music school. Van Blinn insisted on meeting me for lunch that day at the country club on Wilshire. Lisa rolled her eyes as I consented.

"Power-over," she snarled, packing her beat up leather messenger bag with notes and books for her classes that day, both the lecture she was attending and the two she'd be teaching that afternoon.

She wore a pair of jeans with a nice colorful sweater over them. I tried to remember when I'd seen the sweater hanging off of her knitting needles and couldn't.

"Whatever." I shook my head and checked my pocket watch. "What time do you need to leave?"

She checked her own watch. "Oh, shavings! Now." She paused. "Are you going to be okay?"

"I'll be fine." I smiled, feeling the warmth of her gaze. "I have you."

She chuckled. "Okay. Why don't you page me when you get done? If I can call, I will."

"I'll do that. Thanks."

We kissed goodbye, then I went back to work on whatever story I was working on that day until I had to leave.

I got to the country club in good time and left my Beemer with the valet. The clubhouse was a touch on the well-worn side - the building had been there since the early teens, as I recall. I'd been there plenty of times before, usually to do an interview with some mover and shaker. Inside was not opulent, but reeked of privilege, power, and maintaining that particular status quo.

I couldn't help chuckling. Stella raised me among a bunch of bohemians, commies, and hippies in San Francisco, and so I don't feel any identification with traditional White Male power structures. Country clubs and all that sort of thing simply do not impress me. If Van Blinn had thought the place was enough to give him the edge in our coming meeting, he was about to be sorely disappointed.

To my surprise, the concierge escorted me immediately to the dining room. Most of the movers and shakers preferred to keep me waiting. The congressman sat at a table for two next to a large window overlooking the driving range, writing in a black-leather bound notebook. As soon as Van Blinn saw me, he shut the book, then rose and shook my hand.

"It is so good to meet you," he said, his watery gray eyes holding steady.

His hands were perfectly manicured and softer than good kid leather. He'd kept all his hair. I was pretty sure it was his because it was flawlessly white. Most guys, if they're going to go to the trouble of wearing a wig, will get it in their former natural color. He stood somewhat taller than me, with narrow shoulders in a soft green polo shirt and tan slacks that did Ralph Lauren proud.

I had put on one of my nicer suits that morning, with a white dress shirt and paisley tie that Lisa had made out of the scraps from one of her dresses. Lisa makes a lot of her clothes and some of mine. She calls it therapy. In any case, if I'd dressed to impress, it had been unconscious. The family frequently gives me crap about being over-dressed. It's what I do.

"Good to meet you," I replied, hoping my tone was nice and non-committal.

"Please sit down." He indicated the menu on the table at my perfectly laid-out place setting. "Feel free to order anything you like."

That's when the penny dropped. The asshole wanted me to like him. Normally, when someone works that hard to get me to like them, I go on guard. But this guy. He wasn't pathetic. He had some sense of his own power, I'll give him that. But while I couldn't figure out why, he definitely wanted me to be friends or something.

I looked over the menu quickly. It hadn't changed appreciably since the last time I'd been at the club. When the waiter came to take our order, I chose the grilled chicken Caesar salad, with water to drink.

"Are you sure you don't want something else?" Van Blinn seemed non-plussed. "Maybe a cocktail?"

I smiled and shrugged. "It's time to get back to eating healthy again."

It was part of the usual January drill for me.

"Oh." Van Blinn ordered a martini for himself along with the hot roast beef sandwich.

I am not a fan of red meat as it is. But even though the sandwich was one of the more popular items on the menu, it was pretty awful. The meat was overdone and dry. The gravy came from a can, and what passed for bread made Wonderbread look edible. {It wasn't that bad. - ljw}

I didn't know what to make of it that Van Blinn looked enraptured when the waiter set it in front of him, but let it go. We hadn't talked much beyond the football play-offs the previous Sunday, neither of which game I'd seen. But professional sports is what guys talk about, so I made a point of being at least conversant about it.

"You don't seem to be much of a football fan," Van Blinn said, after tasting his sandwich.

"I'm not," I said. "My son, however, has a passing interest this year. He's a 'Niners fan."

Not much of one, admittedly, since Nick lives and breathes baseball, and specifically, the San Francisco Giants. He lived in the Bay area until he was 12, when his first, or birth, mother died, and Lisa and I took custody of him.

Van Blinn's eyebrows lifted. "You have a son?"

I smiled. "Yeah."

"How old is he?"

"Fifteen," I said.

Van Blinn sighed. "That's amazing."

"It is." I didn't elaborate.

"You have no idea how lucky you are," Van Blinn said, blinking his watery eyes, then touching his notebook.

"I know how lucky I am," I said, but again, chose not to elaborate on how Lisa had made my relationship with Nick possible.

"Yes, I see." Van Blinn smiled. "You've obviously made something of yourself."

My eyes narrowed. "I'm not sure I understand you."

"Well, look at how well you're turned out. You've clearly made some significant money."

"Not entirely. I started with a good inheritance from Sheila's father," I said.

"That's impossible." Van Blinn's eyes blinked rapidly. "Sheila didn't have any money."

"She was born into it."

"But then why...?" Van Blinn looked at me quizzically. "You're a strange one, son."

I couldn't help it. I glared at him, then held up my hands.

"Let's get one thing clear," I said. "I am not your son."

"You damned near were." Van Blinn sat up straight, looking utterly affronted.

That got me. "What's that supposed to mean?"

He looked away, then back at me. "I was going to marry your mother."

It took me a second to realize who he meant. "Sheila?"

"Of course. Who else?" He stroked the notebook again.

"Hm." I looked at my salad. I was still having trouble thinking of Sheila Hackbirn as a real person, let alone as the woman who had given birth to me.

"She and I were in love," Van Blinn continued.

"How did you two meet?" I had to ask.

Van Blinn cleared his throat. "At Jane Smith's house. I was, eh, a client there. All of us boys in the firm were. I was newly graduated from law school, had just passed the bar. I was expected to make partner, which meant participating in the fun and games. The one boy I knew who didn't, well, his career was ruined. They called him gay and he ended up clerking in the public defender's office, I believe."

"But if you were going to marry Sheila, wouldn't your co-workers have known she was a hooker?" I frowned.

"One of the partners was going to help me to my happiness." Van Blinn huffed. "More than likely he wanted something he could hold over my head. It's how things operate sometimes." He shook his head. "It didn't matter. I was young and in love. Your mother was an amazing woman. Absolutely beautiful, with that delightful Southern charm. And intelligent. She was a brilliant strategist. She even helped me win my first court case. I'm sure her sister didn't tell you about how wonderful your mother was."

"Actually, Stella told me how smart she was." I poked at the greens on my plate, feeling seriously nettled.

Van Blinn snorted. "She never understood your mother."

"How well did you know Stella?"

"Never met her." Van Blinn sat up. "Never wanted to. My darling Sheila had nothing good to say about her older sister. That woman was cold and cruel."

"And also gave up her life to raise me," I said softly, glaring at him.

"Are you sure about that?" His eyebrows rose.

"Pretty damned," I replied.

Well, I may have been speaking with a little more confidence than I felt. But then, I'd heard parts of the story that I was reasonably sure Van Blinn knew nothing about. Most of it was from Stella's perspective, true, but there had been other hints that when I thought about it later, supported a lot of what Stella had told me.

"Sheila said that her sister was a big liar." Van Blinn shuddered. He touched the notebook again. "And that her sister had forced her into hustling."

That kind of got to me because it was sort of true. According to Stella, what she'd actually told her younger sister was that if Sheila was not going to take care of me, then she'd better go out, get a job, and support the three of us. Stella had bought Sheila's story that she was working at an import company at night because that's when they needed somebody to take phone calls and wires from overseas.

The funny thing was, Stella had known Sheila had been prostituting herself when she got pregnant with me, so why hadn't she questioned the night job? I made a mental note to ask Stella about that.

"You just said that you never met Stella," I said, crossly. "What makes you so sure that Sheila told you the truth?"

"I knew her!" Van Blinn glared at me. "You did not."

"No, I didn't." I glared at my plate then at him. "But I know Stella. I know what finding out about that room has done to her."

"You know nothing about Sheila."

"And do you know her real name?" I sat back and folded my arms.

"She told me. Hackbirn. Like yours."

I shook my head. "No. It wasn't. And I don't just have Stella's word on that."

Van Blinn licked his lips, then blinked at me. I suddenly figured out why he wanted me to like him, and it really pissed me off.

"Look, congressman," I said, glaring at him. "I don't know what happy little fantasy you cooked up for yourself, and I don't give a fuck."

"Your mother—"He jabbed his forefinger at me.

"Get this straight." I jabbed back. "My mother is the woman who actually raised me. That's what counts. And I do not appreciate you running her down, especially when you don't even know her."

"But, son—"

"I'm not your son!" I snapped. "And if you were so fired up about becoming my dad, why didn't you reach out to Stella? Why didn't you try to find us?"

"I— I—" Van Blinn licked his lips again. "My family. It was so difficult." He suddenly sighed. "And there were those who were happy to believe that I had killed your mother. I didn't! I swear I didn't!" He blinked and licked his lips. "I was scared." He looked up at me, pleading. "And I was devastated. I loved Sheila, from the very depths of me, and she was gone. My little family. Gone."

I knew I was supposed to be investigating him. I knew he was still feeling the hurt of thirty-seven years before. But I just couldn't take it anymore. I pushed my salad away and stood up.

"Congressman, thank you for lunch, but I've got to get going."

I looked back at him. He had caved in on himself.

"Oh, dear." He blinked his eyes and stroked his notebook. "Maybe I did presume too much."

"Yeah. You did." I swallowed. He would have no way of knowing that it was my sweet Lisa's influence on me, but I decided to throw him a bone. "Look. You seem like a decent enough guy. And, okay, I can't just go along with this little scenario of yours. But if you're willing to accept that there may be parts of this story that Sheila didn't tell you or even lied about..." I took a deep breath. "Then, I guess I can accept that maybe Stella didn't tell me everything, either."

"Oh." He frowned, then looked up at me. "I— I— Yes. That would make sense. I'm sorry I was so hard on Sheila's sister. Of course, you would accept her word on what happened. Why wouldn't you? I accepted what your mother told me."

"Fine. Then keep in touch."

I turned and left. As I entered the building foyer, my hand slid to my inside breast pocket and the transmitter there. I handed the valet my ticket.

"Here you go," I said, not so much for the valet's benefit, but for the other person listening in.

"Got you, Big Red," said the voice in my ear.

My Beemer showed up promptly, and I passed the valet a generous tip. I waited, though, until I was headed down the club driveway to talk into my transmitter.

"You came in loud and clear, Red Dawn." I sighed. "Couldn't get the tracker placed directly on the subject, though. He was wearing slacks and a polo shirt."

"Them's the breaks. I got the car he's using wired, so Red Gate can monitor from a distance."

As I got to Wilshire Boulevard, I saw Red Dawn, or Jesse White, in a white van with the yellow and blue logo of a security company parked near the entrance of the club, where he could see the driveway, but far enough away that no one would question it sitting there.

"Good," I said as I turned right onto Wilshire and headed back toward Mid-City, where Stella's music school was. "We don't want too tight a tail on the subject, unless Red Sky pulls up something interesting in his financials."

"Roger that." Jesse's voice chuckled. "I'll check in with you guys later. Maybe you can find a keychain he keeps on him or something, if we need to go tighter."

"We'll see. Over and out."

January 10, 1989

(Lisa's Voice)

I was so crazed that morning. I'd been dreading that semester as it was. Yes, I was excited about my classes, but my meetings the day before had only confirmed my worst fears - all three of my PhD classes were going to be incredibly time-consuming and challenging.

Since I'm required to teach as part of my program, I had a Basic Comp class at a local community college. Only right before Christmas, the department chair there had twisted my arm into taking a second section of Basic Comp.

Also, right before Christmas, Mama had dropped a bit of a bombshell on me. My cousin Maggie, at my mother's direction, had also enrolled at the community college where I taught. Maggie had moved to Los Angeles from Florida the September before, having been transferred when the company she worked for had been bought out. The two of us had moved past the open hostility we'd shared in our youths. But we were not going to be friends. She still thought I was a horrible snob, and I could not stand the way she flirted with Sid, as if she was going to steal him from me.

Not that she had a hope in hell of succeeding. I had a feeling Maggie may not have even been that serious about it. But it sure made meetings with her uncomfortable as all get out. Even Sid, who flirts outrageously just for the fun of it, was getting creeped out by Maggie.

And on top of it all was the nuisance job, including what it meant for Sid and Stella. I was worried about both of them. Sy had taken over caring for Stella. Sid had gotten through the night before without any nightmares, for which I thanked God. After our meeting with Lillian and Henry, Sid and I set up basic surveillance on Van Blinn with our team and good friends, Jesse, Kathy, Frank, and Esther. Kathy was already digging into Van Blinn's financial records, while Jesse would find Van Blinn's car at the country club and install a tracker on it so that Frank could monitor Van Blinn's movements. Esther would take over monitoring once she got back the next day from the Consumer Electronics Show in Las Vegas.

Which meant that all six of us would be spending more time than we wanted following a probably harmless old man around while trying to lead normal lives because no one, but no one, is supposed to know that we're all six of us undercover operatives for a top-secret counter-espionage agency.

It didn't help that Advanced Curriculum, my one lecture class, turned out to be as much about dealing with politics as it was about trying to figure out what students needed to learn. Which makes sense. Most school boards are made up of politicians, and a lot of them don't have any educational background. But it was not what I wanted to be dealing with.

Then, as I left the classroom, one of my advisors caught me in the hallway and wanted an extended chat. Then there was a line at the bookstore, where I needed to buy the extra textbook for Advanced Curriculum. By the time I got out of there, I barely had forty-five minutes to get to the community college where I was teaching.

I stopped at the cheap taco place in desperation since I'd forgotten my lunch that morning. While waiting in the drive-through, I called Frank from my car phone to find that the tracker had been installed on the car the subject had arrived in at the country club earlier that morning, and it was functioning.

"I'm getting a reading," Frank said. "Jesse says that Sid left around twelve-forty-five, but the subject hasn't gone anywhere."

"Thanks," I said, then hung up.

That Sid had left after only forty-five minutes did not bode well. I tried calling his car but didn't get through. He'd either already arrived at Stella's music school, which seemed likely given how close it was to two o'clock, or one of us was in a dead zone for the cell phone signal.

I glanced at the clock on my dashboard and almost cried, but pulled into the faculty lot at the college with barely ten minutes to spare before my first class. I rushed through the department office to get my class sheets, then ran for the classroom. At least that class went reasonably well.

The other bright spot in my day was that Nick showed up at my classroom just as I dismissed the other students. Nick is what's called a bridge student, which means that he's taking classes for credit at the college while still in high school. He's very gifted, especially in chemistry, and was too advanced in that subject even for the very challenging program that his high school has. The main reason I'd chosen that college to teach at was because it would make driving him around easier, although Nick usually took the bus from his high school to the college.

"Hey, my sweet guy." I grinned and played with the lock of hair that always falls over his forehead. "How was school?"

"Okay. Mostly the usual." He shrugged. "I got a note home, though." He made a face. "I'm supposed to shave every day now."

Nick goes to a Catholic all-boys school and is also not allowed to wear his hair past his collar or facial hair. I'd been wondering when the school's teachers were going to question the dark wisps covering his chin and cheeks.

"Your father will be thrilled." I chuckled.

Sid had been itching to do something about Nick's beard for a while but had been biting his tongue in an attempt to let Nick make his own decisions. Which, naturally, meant that Nick was totally onto him and had been not-so-subtly resisting his father's equally not-so-subtle attempts to get him to clean up.

Nick made a face. "Well, I knew I was going to have to." He shrugged. "I'm okay with it."

Smiling, I shook my head. I had a feeling Nick had changed his stance on shaving simply because most of his peers couldn't yet.

Unfortunately, chit-chatting almost made both of us late to our respective classes. Nick's was across the quad in the science building. Mine was up another floor and down the hall. As I raced into the room, I thought I heard a groan. Then, as I dumped my leather bag on the desktop and looked over the group of students, I realized I had.

I must concede the person who groaned had good reason for her dismay. I was equally dismayed when I finally looked at my class sheet and saw Caulfield, Margaret, among the student names.

"I'm Lisa Wycherly," I announced. "And this is English One-A, Basic Composition. I'm your teacher. Is everybody sure they're in the right place?"

The students did the usual shuffle, including my cousin Maggie, who also shot me an evil glare. I smiled at her, then took roll, asking the students to tell me if they had a preferred nickname. When I called Margaret Caulfield, she looked at me funny.

"I go by Maggie," she said.

"Maggie it is," I said, making a note.

I finished with roll call, then went through the basic course requirements. The next part of class was a brief getting to know you session, where each student introduced his or her self. The room was too small and too full for everyone to put their chair/desk combos into a circle. So everyone sat in their rows. They were mostly freshmen, and mostly fresh out of high school, but this being a somewhat later class, a good quarter of the students were older. Some were coming back to college after an absence. Others had found they needed the degree, after all. And some, including Maggie, had never had the opportunity to go.

"It's something I've always wanted to do," she said defiantly. "Most of my family said I didn't need to go to college. That I could get by on my looks. And I wasn't smart enough, anyway."

"Well, that's bull-puckey." It slipped out of my mouth before I realized what I'd said. "You're plenty smart."

Maggie looked at me. The truth is, she is very beautiful and always has been. Her father is my mother's older brother, and while that side of the family tends to be short and round, Maggie had gotten her mother's more willowy frame. True, her blond hair had always had some help from a bottle, and I could see some dark roots among the highlights in the hair that she'd cut short sometime after I'd last seen her the previous fall.

I flushed a little, then smiled. "I'm sorry you had to hear that."

She quirked her head. "Anyway, that's why I'm here, and I'm a business major."

We moved on. I gave out the first assignment, which was done in class. Maggie held back after I dismissed the class and collected the papers as the other students left.

"You really think I'm smart?" she asked once we were alone.

"Yeah." I looked at her quickly, then focused on gathering papers together.

"How the hell did you get that idea?"

I shrugged. "It's the way you talk about things. Like when you were practicing for beauty pageants, you thought about the judges and why you wanted to present yourself one way or another."

"But you thought beauty pageants were stupid."

"True." I flushed a little and winced. "But I only said so because I was, what? Seven at the time?"

Maggie chuckled. "I suppose that's fair enough." She paused, then frowned. "How come you pretended like you didn't know me today?"

"Well, I didn't know you were going to be in the class."

"I didn't know you were teaching it. The class schedule just said Staff."

I smiled. "That's right. I was assigned the class right before Christmas, so they didn't have time to get my name in the schedule." Shrugging, I made a face. "I didn't know what you wanted me to do. Sometimes, students get weird when it's obvious one of their classmates knows the teacher. I didn't want to embarrass you."

Maggie thought that over, then nodded. "Lisa Wycherly, I am never going to get you."

"Hey, Mom." Nick scurried into the room. "I'm done."

Maggie's grin grew sharp. "Well, if it isn't that sweet bit of sugar you got."

"Maggie," I snapped. "He's fifteen."

Maggie rolled her eyes and sauntered from the classroom.

"Man, she's creepy." Nick shuddered.

"I know." I double-checked to make sure I had all my stuff.

"At least Dad's not here. Blech. That was way gross."

"I agree." I sighed and looked at my son. "But I think that's the only way she knows how to be."

Sid paged me as Nick and I walked to my little dark blue Datsun pickup. As I pulled out onto the street, I called Sid's car phone and found that not only had he picked Darby up from orchestra practice, Sy and Stella would join us for dinner that night.

"How is she?" I asked.

"Still in a crappy mood," Sid replied. "She yelled at Tyeesha today."

"Oh, no."

Tyeesha is a sweet kid and very talented. But at twelve years old, she can be a little on the rowdy side. Stella's patience with her is phenomenal. Or had been.

"Stella apologized, but still..." Sid sighed deeply. "She wants to hear about my meeting with Van Blinn."

"How'd she find out about that?"

"I told her that I'd talked to him. One of my more colossal mistakes."

"Lover, you're doing the best you can," I said, even though I agreed that he had made a doozy.

I heard Darby in the background, then Sid growling at him. Oh, goody. Stella wasn't the only one in a crappy mood.

Sy and Stella had already arrived, as had Sid and Darby, when I pulled my little truck into the garage. Conversation at dinner was pretty banal, then I sent the boys off to do their homework before time for bed. For once, neither complained about having to do it, although Darby sighed loudly.

Darby had been staying with Sid, Nick, and me during the week since the boys had started high school. Ostensibly, it was an easier way to get him to school and violin lessons and everywhere else he needed to be. But I honestly think it had more to do with keeping Mae and Neil from pounding him into oblivion. Not that they would, but adolescents can make you want to.

As soon as the boys had left the table, Stella glared at Sid.

"So who is this Van Blinn character, and why is he important to Sheila's murder?"

"He said that he was going to marry her." Sid shifted. "He was a client at Jane Smith's house, claimed it was an office thing. But he said that he fell in love with Sheila and that he was going to be my father."

"Oh." Stella huffed. "Maybe she wasn't lying after all."

"I suspect not," Sy said, reaching over and stroking Stella's arm.

Stella looked at Sid. "She said that she had found someone to take her away and that she was going to take you with her." Stella blinked and shook her head.

"We did not doubt that she was going away," Sy grumbled. "It was only a matter of time before she did."

"She wasn't going to take Sid," Stella snapped. "She wouldn't have. She didn't give a crap about him!"

Sid shook his head. "But apparently, Van Blinn did. He was convinced that I was going to fall all over myself, embracing him as my surrogate father."

"But she slapped you. And she left you alone!" Stella pressed her lips together and shuddered. "It happened all the time. She swore she would watch you and take care of you, and she didn't!"

"My darling," Sy said. He pulled away from her physically, though. "It is entirely possible that if this Van Blinn wanted a ready-made family, then Sheila might have seen Sid as her ticket out from underneath your thumb."

"She was never under my thumb!" Stella yelled. "Why would you say that?"

"That was her perception," Sy said calmly. "It doesn't matter that it was not, in fact, the case. She believed it to be. And we both know that."

Stella looked at her nephew. "The only thing I did to her was insist that she get a job to support her son. And me, so that I could take care of you, Sid. Or I'd tell Father where to find her. I swear that's all I did."

"I believe you," Sid said quietly. "But why did you believe her when she told you that she worked at an import company?"

Stella closed her eyes and lowered her head. "I didn't. I tried to tell myself that she wasn't turning tricks. But I was fairly certain that she was. I just couldn't confront her without hard proof. The few times I tried, Sheila raised hell with me. And with justification. I didn't actually know what she was doing." Stella's breathing grew labored. "And it was such a shock to find out I was right. You see, I didn't really want to know. I couldn't change her." She looked over at Sid. "It was, ultimately, her choice. And it didn't matter. We had a good roof over our heads, food on the table, and I was able to take care of you. That was the most important thing. That I was able to take care of you. I hope you understand that."

Sid closed his eyes for a moment, then smiled. "Yeah, Stella, I do. I don't know if I would have a few years ago. I like to think that I would. But..." He looked back toward Nick's room. "I certainly do now."

Sy reached over and laid his hand gently on Stella's shoulder.

"My darling, it is, perhaps, time we made our way to our home," he said.

"It is high time that we found out what happened to my sister," Stella snarled.

"However, we will not be able to do it tonight," Sy replied firmly. He looked over at Sid. "You will keep us abreast of any discoveries that you make?"

"I will," Sid said. "I hope you'll share any information you get with me."

"Without question." Sy got up and pulled Stella to her feet. "Come, my darling. Let us sleep on what we have learned and ponder the rest of it tomorrow."

Sid and I led Sy and Stella out of the house, giving them both hugs and kisses. I went to check on the boys, who had finished their homework and begged me to let them watch TV until their nine o'clock bedtime. That they didn't need to beg was irrelevant. Chuckling, I returned to the office to start grading papers from earlier that day and maybe get some reading work done.

We have a fire safe built into one of the cabinets in there, where we keep things like our passports, my aquamarine necklace and earrings, and the few records we have on the business. Sid stood next to the open safe door, looking at a file folder.

"What are you looking at?" I asked, walking over to him.

"My life papers," he said, closing the safe's door while still holding the file. He went over to his desk and reopened the file. "My mother's picture."

"Are you finally thinking of getting it framed and put out?" I smiled. I'd been trying to nudge him in that direction for years.

"Nah." He sighed and shook his head, still gazing at the black-and-white photo.

I'd always thought that it was a gorgeous shot and still marveled at how much the young woman with the bright, light-colored eyes looked like Stella must have back then. While the cleft in her chin made Stella look more stern, the gentle dimple in the photo simply added to the young woman's allure.

Sid, however, insisted on keeping the photo in the file, claiming that it had little to no meaning to him, certainly not enough to justify a place on our increasingly crowded walls. I would have thought he was being weird about it except that he didn't mind taking it out and showing it to me, Nick, or one of the other kids.

"Nothing's changed," he said that evening. "That photo, itself, still doesn't mean that much. If it didn't look so much like Stella, I probably wouldn't have kept it."

Still, he pulled the photo from the file containing his birth certificate and a few school records. Leaving the photo on the desk, he put the file back in the safe, closed the door and twirled the knob. Going back over to the desk, he sighed as he gazed at the photo.

"I was hoping that looking at it again would help make her more real to me," Sid said finally.

"And?" I asked. "Is it working?"

He shrugged. "Not really. Maybe it will just take a little time."

January 11, 1989

If I wasn't exactly paying attention when Sid took a call the next morning, it was because I was hip deep in grading Basic Comp papers. It had been a frantic morning, with Sid trying to show Nick how to shave. They both gave up before too much blood was shed. Sid wrote a note for Nick, explaining that shaving around Nick's cleft chin was not something that could be learned while rushing to get ready for school.

I was thrilled to be focusing on something besides family angst when the call came through. Sid picked up the handset, so I only heard his side of the conversation, which was the usual greeting, then lots of hmms and hahs. He also typed several names and phone numbers into a file on his computer, which is why I didn't pay any attention initially.

"Well, thanks, Jay," Sid said, and I looked up. "If you can give me whatever information you get on the contacts on your end of the country, I'd appreciate that... I'd be happy to work with you on the story. I, uh, would just rather keep my personal connection out of it... There's that, but it's, uh, Stella. As you can imagine, she's not dealing too well with this. I think she could use some privacy, if you know what I mean..." Sid laughed. "Okay. Well, thanks again. I'll keep you up to date with what I find out."

He hung up and looked at me.

"What's that about?" I asked.

He made a face. "Jay Fedders. That research he's been doing on the women listed in the ledger. He told us about it at lunch that first day. Remember?"

I thought for a moment. "Not really."

"Well, he got it organized today and suggested that the two of us work together on a story about the case. There are eight women in the ledger, right?"

"Uh, yeah."

Sid rolled his eyes and smiled at me. "Well, three of the former hookers now live out here in Southern California. Four are on the East Coast. And the last passed away about four or five years ago. Anyway, Jay said that he'd talk to the ladies on his side of the country. But he asked me to talk to the three that are here, plus Jane Smith's daughter."

"Smith. That was the madam, wasn't she?"

"Yeah." Sid nodded. "And that was her real name, too, apparently. That's one of the twists in the case. Within a week or two after the murder, Smith sold the house and moved to Los Angeles, supposedly because her daughter had a deal with one of the movie studios. Or maybe she got the deal after they got here. Jay isn't sure which. But the daughter did get one and made quite a career. Her name is Hannah Davis."

My eyebrows rose. "I have no idea who she is."

"Definitely on the B-list." Sid chuckled, referring to Davis's status in Hollywood. He went over to our office bookshelf and pulled the movie almanac off it. He flipped through the pages, then raised his eyebrows. "Looks like Jay wasn't exaggerating. She's been working pretty steadily since Fifty-three."

"Wow. Does it say how old she is?"

"Born in January 'Forty-three." Sid shrugged. "Even odds that's true. So, she would have been nine or ten when Sheila was killed."

"I wonder if she remembers it."

"I guess we'll find out."

"What about Jane Smith?" I frowned as I bit my lower lip. "It seems to me that she'd remember something."

"If she were alive." Sid replaced the almanac. "Jay said that's what Davis told him when he talked to her a few months back. And hung up right after that without saying much more."

"What?" I couldn't help chuckling. "Davis didn't want to talk about her mother's infamous past? Who knew?"

Sid chuckled, too. "Still, we should probably look up the death certificate and verify it."

"Probably." I looked over my papers. "Who else have we got?"

"Rhoda Farber, Tina Goetz, and Earline Spinner." Sid slid back into his desk chair and frowned at the screen. "I've got phone numbers for Farber, Goetz, and Davis. Jay said that Spinner didn't come up when he called directory assistance for the California area codes. Or when his intern did."

"Then how does Jay know that Spinner came out here?" I frowned at the paper in front of me. The student's hand-writing was worse than Sid's, and his is pretty awful.

"One of the other women, a Miranda Stoddard, kept in touch with some of the others. Not sure why. Jay said that he got the impression from Stoddard that Jane Smith was very protective of her girls. And come to think of it, there is emergency contact information for almost every woman in the ledger, including Stella."

"Another way to find them?"

Sid shook his head. "Jay already tried. That's how he got to Stoddard. But most of the contact people have long since died. Or the woman remained cut off from her family."

I studied him, but again his face was not readable. "You okay?"

He shrugged. "Okay enough."

I looked at him again, but then Conchetta Ramirez came in with the mail. She's our housekeeper, about medium height, with gray-streaked black hair she generally wears in a long braid down her back. That morning, she had on a gray hooded zip-front sweatshirt over a black long-sleeved t-shirt featuring the latest Ramones tour. Conchetta has an incredible collection of hard rock and heavy metal t-shirts, mostly from concerts she's been to.

"You got a package today," she told Sid, handing him the large, flat box with the FedEx logo on it.

Conchetta picks up our mail from the rental box every morning before she comes in.

"Thanks," said Sid with a smile.

Conchetta shrugged and left without another word. She's pretty cantankerous, especially when we get friendly with her. Unfortunately, thanks to her previous employers, she has good reason to be. Sid grabbed the letter opener out of the pencil cup next to his computer and went to work on the box.

"Is that what I think it is?" I asked, sighing as I looked at the stack of papers still to be graded.

"It's got Reilly's name on it," Sid said, struggling a little as he got the box open.

When the last of the tape fell away, he pulled out a black three-ring binder, three inches thick and stuffed with paper, and a manila envelope full of black and white photos.

"Wow," I said.

"This is it, alright." Sid thumbed through the photos, then opened up the binder. "Looks like there are notes here on everyone Reilly, Senior, interviewed." He fell silent as he read. "Huh. Looks like Van Blinn was their number one suspect."

"Hm." I frowned. "And what do you think?"

Sid winced. "Well, we both know that when cops focus in on a suspect, it's more often than not with cause. The problem is, I just didn't get that guilty feeling from him. Which means he either has so thoroughly convinced himself of his innocence, he doesn't act guilty, or he didn't do it."

"And if he did, does that have any effect on what we're supposed to be looking at him for?"

"Who knows?" Sid rolled his eyes, shook his head, then looked back at the binder. "I suspect that we might have to say something if it becomes obvious he once literally got away with murder. Or maybe not. At this point, it's not up to us, especially without some solid evidence, which we do not have."

"True." I looked at the stack of papers again and sighed.

"You okay?"

"It's just that I'd rather be looking at that casebook than grading papers. But if I don't stay on top of the papers, I'll be drowning in no time, not to mention my other courses." I shut my eyes. "I'm glad I'm doing this. I really am. But I'm also having one of my 'what am I doing?' moments."

Sid laughed. "I believe it. But like you kept telling me when I got stressed out over my masters work, it will be worth it in the long run."

"You're right." I glared at the papers again, then took a deep breath. "Okay. Let me burn through these, then maybe I can spend an hour reading the case book before I do my reading for tomorrow's class. Oh, and I've got to go to the copy store, too, sometime today."

The phone rang again, and in deference to me, Sid grabbed it.

"Uh-huh," he grumbled. "Yeah, I got it... I know, but, Stella, we're not cops. We have to believe that someone out there got away with murder a lot of years ago and is not going to be happy about us poking around. And if he already killed once... Yes, I do want to know. And I totally understand why you do... Well, excuse me if I want all of us to come out of this alive..." He sighed deeply. "I'll get you the copies. Do you want the photos, too...? Fine... I'll talk to you later."

He slammed the phone down.

I looked up at him. "She wants to see the casebook, doesn't she?"

"She wants full copies." Sid groaned and got up from his desk to pace. "She doesn't get it. This is dangerous."

"I know." I closed my eyes. "But we are sort of like cops."

"BFD," Sid said. Okay, he did not use the acronym. "Fedders gave her the same list of contacts he just gave me. What the hell was that idiot thinking?"

"The same thing that Jane Reilly is thinking? The more eyes on this, the better?" I made a face. "He may even have a point. And if we share what we have with Stella, what are the odds we can keep tabs on her and keep her out of trouble?"

"How about nil? Zip. Zero." Sid shuddered. "Plus, we've got Van Blinn to worry about."

"Sid, she got the same information from Fedders that we did. You know she'll get into bigger trouble if we don't work with her."

Sid's language got exceptionally foul, even for him, and his pacing grew faster.

"And I can't tell her I won't get the casebook copied for her." He cursed again. "I should have. I don't know why I didn't."

"It doesn't matter." I got up and pulled him into my arms. "Even if you had told her no about the copy, she would have found some other way to get the casebook. Let's be thankful that we've got the skills to keep her as safe as can be."

"You're right," he said, squeezing me tightly.

"Let me get through these papers while you're reading the casebook. Then I'll take it to the copy store. I've got copying to do anyway." I put my hands up as Sid sighed. "You know I'd buy the book if I could. But the student bookstore says that it's out of print, and there don't seem to be any used copies anywhere. So I'm stuck with the library copy, and they're not going to let me mark it up and keep it all semester. And what if I need it for my dissertation?"

"I get it." Sid pulled me close to him. "Why don't I help? It will go faster and be more interesting, anyway."

"Fine."

We kissed lazily but then had to go back to work. I was done grading just in time for lunch. After Sid and I ate, we headed to the copy store, where we went to work copying both the casebook and Jane Smith's ledger, and then the book that I needed for my project on teaching Shakespeare's more awkward plays for modern audiences, such as Othello and Taming of the Shrew. I finished with the book first, then grabbed the copies of the ledger and started feeding them into the copy machine. Sid was waiting for more change.

"Sid," I said as he came back to the machine next to me. "I just had a couple of thoughts. Didn't Van Blinn say he was staying with a friend named Earline?"

Sid frowned as he fed quarters into the machine. "You know. I think you're right."

"Earline Spinner was one of the people that Fedders couldn't get a phone number for. She would almost have to be the friend that Van Blinn was talking about."

Sid made a face. "Which means we're going to be talking to Van Blinn again. I can't wait."

"And here's something else." I held up a sheet from the ledger. "That code. You want to try and crack it? Or we could send it up to San Francisco."

We have a code expert living there.

"That's a good question." Sid shook his head. "Why don't we hold off? We also have a cover to keep intact. It wouldn't be good to know too much about that sort of thing."

Nick was home from school when we got back to the house. He told us that Sy and Stella would bring Darby home from the music school after his violin lesson.

"What's going on with your homework?" I asked, sorting papers out on my desk while Nick hung in the office doorway.

"I gotta study for a biology test," Nick said, smoothing out the two Band-Aids on his chin from that morning's shaving lesson.

"Uh-huh." Sid chuckled and looked at his son with some skepticism.

Nick, being very gifted in the sciences, doesn't usually need to work that hard.

"Well, I do need to go over my notes," he said, grinning.

"And what else do you have?" I asked.

"An essay on Merton for religion." Nick didn't quite roll his eyes. His class was reading New Seeds of Contemplation by the monk Thomas Merton.

"I liked that book," I said.

Nick sighed. I couldn't blame him. When you're fifteen, almost sixteen, and your mother is more excited about one of your textbooks than you are, it can be tough to take. Sid smiled and shook his head. He's an atheist because that's how Stella raised him, having lost her own faith in the Catholic Church thanks to her father's abuse.

"What else?" Sid asked.

"Reading to do for English." Nick heaved the sigh of the utterly beleaguered. "And questions for History. It's, like, so boring!"

I smiled at him. "But it's an important part of being conversant in our common culture, not to mention understanding where we've been helps us to avoid making the mistakes of the past."

"Mom!" At that moment in time, no teen boy was half as put upon as my darling son.

"Nick, go do your homework," Sid said, smiling.

Our boy made a face. "I have to before Darby gets home anyway. I've got to help him with his geometry homework. And he promised to help me with my essay."

"Then hop to it," said Sid.

Nick slumped off. Sid watched him go with a look of utter satisfaction.

"I needed that," Sid said.

"What do you mean?"

"There was just something so incredibly, wonderfully normal about that exchange just now." He slid into his desk chair. "Honestly, Lisa? I cannot believe how much I love that little squid."

Um. He didn't say squid.

"He's not so little," I said, laughing.

Nick was almost six feet tall at that point and taller than either Sid or me.

"Nope." Sid laughed. "Who knew I was going to come to such a bad end?"

That's when the phone rang. Sid picked it up, said yes a couple of times, then held his hand over the mouthpiece of the handset.

"Jesse and Frank have a report for us," Sid said quietly. "They want to come over."

"Sure," I said. "The whole crew?"

Meaning Jesse and Frank's wives, Kathy and Esther, plus Jesse's toddler son, Keshon.

"Nah," said Sid. "Keshon's got a cold, and Kathy says she's getting it, too. And Esther got in late last night from Vegas, so she wants to keep watching for movement on Van Blinn."

"Okay."

Frank and Jesse arrived on our doorstep within twenty minutes and sat with us in our office with the door shut.

"Esther's fancy tracker seems to be working," said Jesse. His skin is the shade of cocoa out of the box, and he keeps his hair in a relatively short but round cut. "I was on the radio with Frank all the way to Newport Beach, and our locations matched. Well, close enough."

"That's good to know," said Sid.

"Anyway, the target landed at a house in a gated community," Jesse continued.

"He hasn't gone anywhere since he got there yesterday," Frank said, yawning and scratching the back of his dark hair. "I took over visual surveillance from outside the gates. There's a road overlooking the house from the back, and I was able to see through the sliding glass door into the room where the target was. He turned out the lights at nine p.m. sharp and went straight to bed, which is when I took off." He winced. "You did say not to stay too tight on him, right?"

"Yeah, we did." Sid smiled at Frank.

"Once I get home, I'll take over monitoring." Frank sat up straight. "Esther wants to go out to the community and check out the electronic security on the tract and maybe the target's house. She thinks she can get the code for the security gate, too."

"But here's the interesting part about that." Jesse leaned back and chuckled. "We may not need that code. I got in today without problem. I told him I had an appointment with a client, and the guard just looked at my ID and waved me through. Didn't write the name down or ask with who."

"That's convenient," I said.

Sid shifted in his chair. "I'm willing to bet that security is a lot tighter at night. We probably won't need it, but it would be good to have that gate code." He glanced over at me. "Why don't I take a turn at visual surveillance tomorrow morning?"

"Oh, and we have a license plate number for you," Jesse said, handing me a slip of paper. "Along with the address on the house."

Sid got up. "Great. Thanks, guys. I'll touch base with both of you in the morning."

Sid and I walked Jesse and Frank to the door. Back in the office, I looked at the paper Jesse had given me.

"I'll have some time between classes tomorrow," I said. "I can go to the library and look up that phone number you have for Van Blinn in the reverse directory." I checked my watch. "It's a bit late for a DMV search on that license plate, though."

"We'll need a case number anyway." Sid sank into his chair and squeezed his eyes shut.

"Are your eyes bothering you?" I asked.

Sid is very near-sighted and wears contact lenses.

"A little." He blinked.

I put my hand on the phone. "I'll call Lillian."

Lillian couldn't give me a case number right away, but said she'd page me when she got one.

Darby hollered that he was home at that moment. Sy and Stella had just dropped him off and didn't come in. It was dinnertime, and the conversation at the table was mostly about the boys' homework and how insanely boring their history teacher was.

After dinner, we all retreated to the library, where the boys usually did their homework unless it needed to be typed. Then they'd retreat to Nick's room, where he had a computer and printer set up. Sid had several magazines he wanted to read. I had my homework reading to do. The boys squabbled quietly as they helped each other, but I only had to remind them not to call each other names a couple of times. All in all, it was a very pleasant evening.

January 12 - 13, 1989

It's a good thing that Sy and Stella had taken Sid and me out to dinner that next evening. I suspect that things would have been even worse had we not been in public.

It had been a largely unremarkable day. Lillian paged me during my morning class. I called her from a pay phone on campus, got the case number, and then hurried to the university library. I found the reverse directory and looked up the phone number that Van Blinn had given Sid.

It belonged to Marlon Wanzyck, and the address matched the one Jesse had given me. I looked Wanzyck up in the regular directory, and there were no other phone numbers for him. I called the DMV's special law enforcement line and got through right away. The license plate record showed the black Cadillac as belonging to Marlon Wanzyck.

I called Sid's car phone after that to let him know. We agreed that it was interesting, but it didn't tell us much about the mysterious Earline. Van Blinn hadn't gone anywhere.

Later, as Sid and I drove to the restaurant where we were meeting Sy and Stella, Sid told me that Jesse was installing a tap on the phone from the outside phone box.

Eduardo Montoya is one of the floaters (or supervisors) for the Blue Line, which is based in Seattle. There are four courier lines for our shadow agency. Ours is red. Montoya's cover career is as a telephone lineman. That fall, he'd agreed to teach members of each of the other lines how to plug into a phone line live from the wire box on the street. Sid, Nick, Jesse, Esther, and Desmond Moore, one of our runners, had all taken lessons.

We started dinner with Sid and Stella going back and forth on the progress of Sid's star pupil, Alicia Mendoza. The thirteen-year-old had only been taking lessons since the year before but was playing better than a lot of accomplished adults. She'd taught herself to play a few years before by listening to the classical music station. The problem was she couldn't read music, and getting her to play a piece without hearing it first was quite a struggle. Sid and Stella were both undecided what to do about it.

We were in the middle of eating when Stella had to ask if Sid had spoken to any of the contacts in the ledger.

"I haven't had a chance to," he grumbled. "It's been busy."

"And I'm not?" Stella said.

We'd gone to Sy's favorite steak house. I was glad because I was able to get a big slab of prime rib, which I love but seldom get because Sid doesn't eat red meat.

Sid sighed and focused on his grilled chicken.

"I managed to talk to Rhoda Farber and Tina Goetz today," Stella continued, pointing her fork at Sid. "I even called Hannah Davis but had to leave a message. I called her twice, even."

Sid's head shot up, his eyes blazing. "You left a message? With what phone number?"

"The school's, of course."

"What the hell were you thinking?" Sid kept his voice down, but that didn't diminish the anger. "You don't know if any of these people are connected to the killer. What if one is and the killer comes after you by chasing down the school's number?"

"How is the killer going to do that?" Stella demanded.

"By looking up the number in a reverse directory. Every library has one. And I'll bet the school's number is not unlisted."

"Of course not." Stella's bright eyes fixed on Sid. "But I've been doing something about this. You haven't done diddly."

"I got you the damned casebook and the ledger."

"Do you mean to tell me that it took your whole morning to copy that?" Stella snorted. "I could have done it in an hour or two in my office."

"I also have writing deadlines," Sid snarled back. "And with Lisa in school, I don't have as much help as I used to."

"You can put aside some time to work on this. It's important."

"I know, Stella." He looked frantically at me. "I'll make some calls tomorrow. In fact, we may have a lead on Earline Spinner. But that's not the issue here. You need to be careful. You don't know who you're dealing with, and you do not have the least idea of how to defend yourself."

"I have enough."

"Do you have a gun?"

"Are you out of your mind, young man?" Stella's voice did rise. "I am a pacifist. I raised you to be a pacifist. We do not carry weapons."

"But what if this killer does?" Sid glanced around quickly. "Do you even know how to tell if someone is following you?"

"Well. I..." Stella sighed, then glared. "What about you? You're not a cop, either."

"I have taken self-defense classes, and Lisa's done several articles on how to keep yourself safe."

"Then you can show me." Stella settled back in her chair with an air of triumph. "And you can start making some of those calls."

Sid looked over at me. "Lisa and I will. Tomorrow." He shifted again. "What did you find out from Farber and Goetz?"

"Not much," Sy said, watching Stella.

"That Goetz woman was just plain disgusting." Stella cut a bite of steak with more force than needed. "Told me she didn't give a damn about what had happened. And that if I knew what was good for me, I'd butt out."

I could see Sid biting his tongue. [Damned near in half. - SEH]

"Sounds not very helpful," I said quickly. "What about Rhoda Farber?"

"Dr. Farber," Stella said derisively. "She wanted me to make an appointment. So I did. For Monday, the twenty-third."

Sid shifted. "Stella, why don't I go with you?"

"Don't you think I can handle it?" Stella's eyes began blazing again.

I jumped in before Sid could. "That's not it at all, Stella." I fumbled for a second. "It will... Uh... Be easier for the two of you to work together if he hears things first hand."

Stella frowned. "True. Very well. Dr. Farber is in San Diego, though." She glared again at Sid. "Are you sure you can find the time to go down there?"

Sid forced a smile. "I will make the time."

Somehow, the four of us finished dinner without any more arguing. But when Sid and I got home, there was a message from Van Blinn on the answering machine inviting Sid to lunch the next day.

"Just what I wanted," Sid grumbled.

It wasn't even eight-thirty. While I went to see where the boys were on their homework, Sid called Van Blinn back.

Sid was still on the phone when I returned to the office.

"Good. I'll see you then," Sid said. "Bye." He hung up and glared at me. "It's convenient as all get out. We're meeting at Wanzyck's place so that I can meet Earline. He still doesn't want to include you for some stupid reason."

"Does it matter?" I slid into my desk chair. "It might make it easier for me to talk to him as one of my alter egos."

As undercover agents, we each have two, both with FBI IDs and civilian ones.

Sid sighed. "Sounds good. Anyway, I want to be sure and thank you for keeping me from jumping down Stella's throat over Farber."

"You're very welcome." I got up and went around my desk to where he sat behind his.

"Crap, she was in rare form tonight." Sid shuddered, then got up. "And poor Sy. What a hell of a time for him to begin living with her."

I squeezed him. "On the other hand, if they survive this, they'll survive anything."

"True." Sid couldn't help chuckling. "My darling, sweet Lisa. You would look at it that way, and I am so very, very glad you do."

I held him again, then looked at my watch. "Well, it's almost nine. How about if you take on chasing the boys to bed, and I go upstairs and read in bed for a bit?"

"How about if I chase the boys to bed, then go upstairs and make you happy?" Sid's grin was less than saintly.

My breath caught. "That sounds nice, too."

(Sid's Voice)

Van Blinn had given me detailed instructions on how to get to the Wanzycks' home, including how to sign in with the guard at the complex gate. I arrived at the complex a little before noon and decided to try the gate code that Esther had gotten for us. It worked. The guard in the shack didn't look at me twice, either.

The house was a large ranch-style, with off-white stucco and dark, rough wood planks. It could barely be seen behind the large bird of paradise and banana plants that ringed the bright green expanse of lawn in front and on either side of the wide driveway in front of the dark brown doors to the three-car garage. Inside, the entryway was paved with shiny terra-cotta tiles hemmed in by a plush off-white carpet on both sides, leading to a dining room on one side and the oversized living room on the other. Everything was laid out meticulously and shone with the kind of glow that meant someone was paying a fortune to maintain it. {Something we have plenty of experience with. - ljw}

I was willing to bet that the woman in her forties who admitted me to the house was not the woman doing the housekeeping. Her honey brown hair was cut into a soft wedge and too perfectly highlighted to be natural. Her stylist clearly knew what he or she was doing and probably charged a small fortune for the privilege. She wore a pink polo shirt tucked into pressed khaki slacks and large diamond stud earrings.

"You must be Mr. Hackbirn," she said softly, leading me to the living room. "I'm Mrs. Marlon Wanzyck. The reverend will be here in a moment. Can I get you anything?"

"I'm fine. Thank you."

"Please have a seat." She waved vaguely at one of the gray leather overstuffed chairs flanking a huge rock fireplace, the diamonds in her wedding ring flashing.

"I'm here to see Congressman Van Blinn," I said, edging slowly toward the chair.

"He'll be out in a minute." She offered me an oddly pained smile.

"You must be Mr. Hackbirn," said a full voice from the back of the living room.

The medium-sized man approaching me moved quickly, but not so fast that I couldn't see the expensively tailored dark gray wool suit and silk tie with blue and white stripes. He shook my hand warmly with both of his, and I saw the edge of a very good toupee that matched his light brown hair perfectly.

"I'm Reverend Marlon Wanzyck," he said, letting go of my hand at just the right angle so that I couldn't miss the huge diamond ring on his right hand. "Please. Sit down. Reba, go tell the congressman that his guest is here."

"Of course, Marlon."

I sat down smiling, but was not happy.

"So." Wanzyck sat down on the chair across from me. "Have you been saved?"

"Um. Yeah."

Yes. I was lying. The last thing I needed was some fuck who had to validate his beliefs by making me believe them, too. Lisa had always said that the only way to keep these bozos off my back was to tell them I believed.

"Great. Where do you go to church?"

I smiled, thinking fast. As it happened, Lisa and I did go to church. She's a practicing Catholic and always has been. I went because I played organ for the choir, not because I believed in it. But odds were decent this guy wouldn't count Catholicism as being saved.

"It's a small community church on the west side of Los Angeles," I said. "Very bible-oriented."

"Oh, for Heaven's sakes, Marlon," said another voice, low and sultry with the slight rasp of a two-pack-a-day habit. It came from the dining room across the entry hall. "You don't have to inspect a religion card for everyone who comes in here."

The woman who'd spoken was a little shorter than Reba, with blond hair in a round helmet glued around her head. Jane Fonda would have envied her body, and she wore dark leggings to emphasize her shape under a frilly, oversized white blouse that opened just enough to allow a glimpse of her cleavage. Her face was far smoother than it should have been, and probably the work of a master surgeon.

Wanzyck rose and cleared his throat. "My... mother-in-law."

I was impressed. She had to be in her early sixties, but looked younger than her daughter.

"I'm Earline Spinner Wilson," she said, sauntering over to me. She didn't smell like she currently smoked cigarettes, never mind the rasp.

I got up quickly. "Nice to meet you."

Her smile grew hot. "Nice to meet you."

Reba scurried in and shot her husband an apologetic look, but didn't say anything.

"So you're Jimmy's guest." Earline slid gracefully onto the couch and daintily crossed her ankles.

"Oh, good, Earline." Van Blinn also came in from the back. "You've met Sid Hackbirn."

"Hackbirn?" Earline's eyebrows raised. That she could said even more about her surgeon. She gazed at me for a moment. "That's right. Sheila had a little boy."

"That was me," I replied softly.

"I'm not surprised." Earline's eyes swept over me. "You look just like her."

"I've been told." Smiling, I let my eyes sweep over her. "How well did you know Sheila?"

Even though I kept my focus on Earline, I heard a gasp from her daughter.

"Well, we weren't friends. We worked together, you know."

"Mother..." Wanzyck's voice was taut.

"Oh, please!" Earline let out a languid titter. "We all know what I did for a living back then. And I have repented. Washed in the blood and all that."

I have never believed in judging others. But I must concede that I couldn't help questioning the sincerity of Earline's penitence. As I took a glance around, I saw that her daughter and son-in-law weren't terribly convinced, either.

"What do you remember about Sheila?" I asked, again turning my focus on Earline.

"It was utterly awful what happened to her." Earline blinked. That I believed she was sincere about. She gazed thoughtfully at me. "You might have had a mother."

"Might have," I said softly.

She laughed. "You're right. Sheila was not exactly the maternal type. She hated kids. She was so mean to poor little Hannah."

I heard a soft sigh from where Van Blinn sat on the couch.

Earline got up, and I rose with her.

"Look, Sid, right?"

"Yeah."

She smiled kindly. "Sheila wasn't a bad person. Like me, she was just stuck in a bad business."

"I don't judge."

"Good." She looked straight at the reverend. "It's the Christian thing to do, right?" She turned back to me. "As for what happened that night, there's not much I can tell you about it. Everyone kept saying it was one of her j— I mean, clients."

"Can you tell us anything about them?"

"There was Jimmy, of course." She smiled and turned away. "And he wasn't the only one sweet on her, by the way. As for the others, it won't do you much good. They're probably dead by now. Except for Jimmy. They were mostly a lot of old men trying to recover lost youth." Turning back, she gave me another appraising gaze. "You had to figure that Sheila's kid was going to be pretty cute. You remind me of her. That same style, finesse."

Van Blinn cleared his throat. "Well, Sid, I think it's time we went to lunch."

"Why don't I drive?" I suggested.

"Yes. Thank you."

Once in the car and headed toward another country club, this one relatively nearby, Van Blinn sighed.

"I'm sorry about the Wanzycks," he said. "They're very nice people. But, as you'd expect, they don't like talking about Earline's past."

"That's not surprising." I frowned. "Wanzyck. I've heard that name before."

"He's pastor of a large evangelical church in Anaheim. Or is it Anaheim Hills?"

"Anaheim Hills," I said, suddenly remembering that I'd read something about him not that long ago. "Living Faith Bible Church. He preaches something called the prosperity gospel, and he got written up... I forget where. My wife didn't think much of him. Or the prosperity gospel."

"What? You don't believe you're wealthy because of your faith?" Van Blinn chuckled.

"Absolutely not. Nor does Lisa. In fact, she says that us having money gives us even greater responsibility to be generous and recognize God's preference for the poor."

"I must concede her point."

"She's good that way." I glanced over at him, then back at the road. "But something Earline said just now. You weren't the only one sweet on Sheila."

"Sadly." Van Blinn shifted. "She had her pick of clients. But I was the one who was going to take her away. I never heard that from the others."

"Such as…?"

He sighed. "Paul West, specifically. I'd rather not have named him. I don't want to get him in trouble. And Earline was right. Most of the clients are dead, and I do not want to sully their memories. On the other hand, somebody is bound to remember Paul's fondness for Sheila. And he is out here in Los Angeles. A tax attorney now. He's one of the people I was going to visit, but I haven't been able to bring myself to contact him." Van Blinn looked at me. "He's not a bad man. None of us were. Or are. We simply needed some female companionship as a way of blowing off steam. You understand that, don't you?"

"I do." And I most certainly did, which got me thinking about Lisa and how we blew off steam. "Um, why didn't you want Lisa to join us?"

He looked astonished. "Why would you want her to come? She'd be bored silly. And we would have to be more… shall we say, refined if she were there."

I just shook my head and didn't bother trying to explain. Men from Van Blinn's background did not want women around, supposedly because women didn't understand or were not interested in the things men talked about. Lisa had said it was all about cutting women out of the deal-making and maintaining the status quo. I glanced back over at Van Blinn. He probably didn't have the least clue that was what he was really doing. But I had to think that Lisa was right.

January 14, 1989

(Lisa's Voice)

I was so glad that Neil had decided to pick up Darby from school that Friday afternoon. When Sid got back from lunch with Van Blinn and fighting his way through Friday afternoon traffic on the 405, he was beat.

He said that lunch itself was pretty boring. However, his meeting with the Wanzycks and Earline Spinner Wilson was pretty strange.

"She said I reminded her of Sheila." Sid winced. "That part wasn't so bad. It's just that I got this weird feeling that Earline didn't like Sheila or something."

"Maybe she was jealous of Sheila. What did Van Blinn say about it?"

Sid rolled his eyes. "Nothing. He just went on another rapturous screed on how wonderful Sheila was. Something tells me this guy did not get Sheila at all."

"Maybe. Maybe not." I scrunched my face up. "He's been living with these memories for a long time. It's always possible he's created a better memory than what actually existed."

"I suppose."

There weren't any more conclusions to be drawn. I'd called Hannah Davis and had left a couple of messages on her answering machine. I could because Sid and I do not have our phone numbers listed in any public directory, and even if they were, we've got them set up so that they're not connected to our addresses.

The next morning, after our usual run, I got dressed and went to teach confirmation class. Sid made good on his word to teach Nick how to shave around the cleft in his chin.

To Breanna, 11/20/2000
Topic of the Day: Being angry
Okay. I guess it's time to work on my anger toward my first mom. Like you say, being angry at her doesn't mean I didn't/don't love her. It just means that it's complicated. Which it is.

The hardest part is getting past the guilt that I was so much happier when Dad and Mom Two took custody of me after Mom One died. But here's the weird thing. Mom One and Grandma always said that I was the best thing that had ever happened to them, only it never really felt like they meant it. It was more like they thought that if they said it enough, they might really feel like I was.

Dad and Mom Two, on the other hand, had never wanted to be parents, nor expected to, but were glad that they were. I remember when Dad taught me how to shave. It was a Saturday morning, and we'd already tried earlier in the week, which hadn't gone well. Shaving that dimple in my chin is not easy.

"I think I got it," I said after scraping away for the fourth time. "Look. No blood."

"Good job." Dad grinned. *He was leaning on the bathroom counter next to me. "Just don't get discouraged when you cut yourself again. Shaving that cleft takes a lot of practice. Stella used to say that she was surprised I had a chin left."*

"She teach you?"

"Uh, no. I had to feel my way around. That's why I'm happy to teach you."

And he was, too. I could see him grinning in the mirror.

"It looks like you're having a lot of fun with this," I said, washing off my face.

"That's because I am."

It just kind of hit me then. "Really? I mean, you didn't want a kid when I showed up."

"I most certainly did not."

I watched him. "Then why did you give me a chance?"

"Your second mom." He laughed a little, then winced. "She knew that I didn't feel all that wanted growing up, and totally leveraged that against me when you arrived on our doorstep."

"But Stella wanted you. A lot."

"I know that now. I just didn't know that growing up." He sighed. "It's always been hard for Stella to express her love for me. She never learned how from her parents. She had a rough time growing up. Her father beat up her mother and her brother and molested her sister. Stella got put down or ignored. That I'm able to express love happened because of your mom, who taught me how, as did Janey, and your Aunt Mae and Uncle Neil, and the rest of the kids. Let's face it, Nick. You and I are insanely lucky in that we found the right kind of people. But we were also smart enough to learn from them. It's a real testament to your mother's love for us that

she married me and adopted you. She wanted us to be a legal family enough that even though she didn't want to be a wife and mother, she became one anyway. And it's why I'm able to be here, getting a kick out of watching you learn how not to scrape your chin to pieces." He reached over and hugged me. "And I am so glad that I am."

Hmm. I wonder if the reason I'm so angry now is that I pushed it back so often, trying to cut Mom One some slack.

Sid and I try not to work on Saturdays and Sundays. It doesn't always work out that way. In the spy biz, you work when things are happening, never mind whether or not it's a weekend.

Most Saturdays during the school year, I teach a class on confirmation, the sacrament most kids receive in their early to mid-teens to affirm that they truly want to be Catholic (never mind that almost all of them are just going through the motions). In our parish, we confirm kids at age fifteen. With Nick's birthday being so early in the year (February), he'd gone through the program the year before, never mind that most kids get confirmed in their sophomore year of high school. So he wasn't with me that Saturday afternoon.

After class, I went over to Esther and Frank's duplex in West Hollywood to put in a shift watching Van Blinn not go anywhere.

Esther sat with me in the back room of the three-bedroom unit. The whole place has a frowzy bachelor pad feel. Even though the monitoring equipment was state-of-the-art and probably pretty expensive, it sat on a beat-up wooden table with two creaky metal office chairs in front of it.

"They have four cars, you know," Esther told me.

"I know. I did the DMV search yesterday," I said, shaking my head. "Three Caddies and a Range Rover."

"Where are they getting the money?" Esther asked, agape.

"According to the article I read a few months ago, it's all from their ministry. He preaches the prosperity gospel. Believe in God and get rich."

Esther snorted. "Hasn't worked for me yet."

"Oh, wait. You have to believe in their version of religion and give them money."

"Maybe I ought to start a new religion."

I laughed.

"Hey. When are we going to do our retreat?" Esther asked.

Almost three years before, the Ladies' Night Out poker party had started as one of the parties before my wedding. But we'd all had so much fun that it had continued and even grown. The annual retreat was actually a trip to Las Vegas, but most of us did some praying, and not just at the tables or slot machines.

"I don't know." I made a face. "It's too late to go this month."

"I told you we should have planned this before Christmas."

"Given this stupid job, it's just as well that we didn't." I glared at the monitor.

Esther looked like she was about to ask, but then realized it wouldn't have done any good. It's how things go with what we do, and at that moment, I was glad. It was getting close to four p.m. when I got a page from Sid to call him at Stella's music school. I called from Esther's secure line, and he asked me to meet him there. He'd seen something that had him... Not happy, I guess.

I told Esther not to worry about Van Blinn for the rest of the night. Truth be told, I was pretty fed up with the whole business and didn't care what the old man was up to. Minutes later, I was in my little dark blue Datsun pickup truck and headed east.

Stella had founded the Sylvester School of Music back in the late '70s in Florida, where she was from. The point of the school was to provide advanced music education to kids who otherwise couldn't afford that kind of training, never mind how much they deserved it. However, in '86, Stella had moved the school to Los Angeles to be closer to Nick and Sid. It was located on Pico, in Mid-City, which made it as accessible as it could be.

Why Sid was there on a Saturday, I did not know. He only taught there on Tuesdays and Thursdays. Stella was usually there on Saturdays. She mostly oversaw the college kids who had come to get some experience teaching in the real world, but she had a couple of students of her own.

I saw what had Sid so concerned as soon as I parked my truck on the street about half a block down from the school. The Cadillac was dark blue, and while I couldn't see who was sitting behind the wheel, someone was. I debated bringing my purse into the school with me, but didn't think I could get away with drawing my Smith and Wesson Model Thirteen revolver. So I dropped the purse behind the driver's seat in the truck's expanded cab.

Sid paced in the front room of the school, which was crowded with four baby grand pianos, music stands and chairs, and a huge bin of sheet music. The college kids had already gone for the day.

"That car across the street?" I asked him softly after a warm hello and a kiss.

"Sy says it's been there all afternoon." Sid adjusted the back waistband of his dark, tight jeans.

He also had on a heather blue sweater with several cable stitches running up and down it over a white dress shirt. Something about the way he hitched his jeans told me that he had his 9 mm automatic in the back waistband holster.

"Is that why you're here?"

"Mm-hmm." Sid looked around. Stella was working with her last student in the back, and Sy was somewhere else in the building. "Sy called me."

"Did either of you get the license plate?"

Sid shook his head. "Neither of us can get close enough without it being obvious that we're looking. The one time I tried, I didn't get across the street before it took off. Then it came right back. Sy said the same thing happened to him."

"That's interesting."

"You said it," said Sid. "I was going to come by anyway and see what I could do to beef up security around here. She won't even lock the doors."

I patted his arm. "We'll convince her to do it."

A young boy, about eleven or so and black-haired, came running out from the back, a stack of sheet music in his hands. His mother followed, talking quietly with Stella.

"Well, the most important thing will be to get Nacho a piano so that he can practice at home," Stella told Nacho's mother.

"Oh, Stella," the woman sighed. "We couldn't. Pianos are so expensive."

Stella snorted. "You wouldn't know that from the way people keep dumping them on me. I barely have room in here as it is. In fact, I have a nice little upright that I can loan you for the time being."

"A loan?" The woman smiled. "That would be nice. I will bring my uncle and his truck. When?"

"How about next weekend?" Stella smiled. "We'll have to get it tuned, though."

Sid shook his head but smiled. "I'll take care of it. Maybe bring Darby with me. He needs some practice working on a piano."

Nacho and his mother thanked Stella several times over, then hurried from the school.

"Well, finally," Stella growled. "Time to close. I tell you, it has been a week."

"Stella." Sy appeared from the office. "You asked me to remind you..."

"About what?"

"Thanking Sid."

"Oh." Stella sighed. She looked over at her nephew. "Thank you for volunteering, Sid."

Sid's eyebrow lifted. "You're very welcome, Stella. Now. We need to think about making this place safer for you. And for your students."

"And why are you assuming that someone is gunning for me?" Stella's blue eyes fixed on him.

"I'm not," Sid growled back. "But you've had problems before. Now, there's the possibility that you've asked the wrong questions of the wrong person. And there is that car outside."

Stella's glare swept over Sy. "You two are worrying about nothing!"

She strode over to the front door and opened it, then waved.

I heard the revving of the engine before I saw the dark car zooming down Pico toward the school. Sid and I glimpsed the barrel in the driver's side window only seconds before the shots cracked. Being closer to the door, I grabbed Stella and pulled her inside. I fell onto the floor with her on top of me. Sid slammed back first into the doorjamb, then rolled, his automatic in his hands. But the car had gone before he could get a shot off, and given how busy the street was, I knew Sid didn't want to risk hitting somebody innocent.

Stella cursed as she tried to roll herself free of my arms and get up. I have no idea how the windows didn't get hit, but I hadn't heard any glass breaking.

"Sy?" Sid called anxiously.

I got Stella straightened out, then rolled over. Sy slowly got to his feet.

"I am untouched," he said, gasping a little. "Stella?"

"I'm fine," she growled, then groaned and cursed some more as she tried to get upright.

I got up and helped her to her feet. She looked at me.

"Are you alright?" she asked me.

I winced, then stretched my back. "I'm okay. Whew! That was scary."

"Yes." Stella blinked, then took a deep breath. "I must concede points to your side." But then she stopped, and her eyes grew wide as she saw the gun in Sid's hand. "What is that?"

Sid holstered the automatic. "My sidearm."

"You are carrying a gun. A deadly weapon!"

"Yeah!" Sid glared her down. "We had someone shooting at us."

"I raised you to be a pacifist." Stella shook in her fury.

"Which went out the window when people started shooting at me!" Sid flat out yelled. "Sorry if I wanted to stay alive."

Stella gaped, then looked at Sy for help.

"My darling," Sy said softly. "He did go to war."

"But..." Stella looked at me, then again at Sid.

"Stella," Sid said, his face creased in pain. "I do not want to be shooting people. I hate it. But I don't want to die either." His eyes squeezed shut, then he opened them. "And I don't want you to die. It is that serious. We just got shot at."

"It doesn't mean it was related to anyone I spoke to." Stella crossed her arms and stared at Sid.

"It's more than likely," Sid snarled, not cowed in the least.

"Even if it was. I would like to think that you still have some respect for the values I taught you!"

"You taught me kindness and respect for all people." Sid began pacing. "Values that, by the way, I am trying to transmit to my son."

Stella huffed. "I did not teach you to carry a gun."

"No. The army taught me that." Sid shuddered. "And you're right. It was the worst mistake of my life. I still feel it. And I hate carrying a gun. But if carrying is going to help keep you alive, then damn it, I am carrying it. Because the greater value for me is you and taking care of you and being there for you. Because you were there for me when I was a kid!"

"Oh." Stella's eyes softened as she looked at him with a bewildered frown. "I can't condone violence, Sid. Even to protect me."

"I understand that," Sid said softly. "And if it were just about me, I might feel the same way. But it's not just about me. It's about you, Sy, Lisa, and Nick. And Darby. And all your students."

Stella took a deep breath. "The one thing I can't argue with." She shook her head. "Very well, Sid. You do what you have to do. I can't condone it, but I can't tell you not to, either."

"Fine." Sid blinked and looked away, then back at her. "I won't tell you to carry a gun or ask Sy to. Sy, if you want to, that's up to you. I'll be happy to train you. But I'm not going to ask you to. That being said, Stella, will you please be more careful? Make sure this place is locked up at night. And I'd also like to have Esther Nguyen install a security system here. You'll be able to get help faster if something bad does happen, and with the right kind of video surveillance, no one will be able to blame one of your kids."

"I do not want to spy on people." Stella crossed her arms again. "And anything I have here belongs to the people, anyway. There's no reason to lock up. Anyone is welcome to take what they want."

"But, Stella, the issue is not about who can take what," Sid said. "The issue is about keeping you and everyone here safe. And no more leaving the number here when you're calling one of the people attached to your sister's case. It makes it too easy for someone to find you who shouldn't. If you have to leave a message..." Sid looked at me, and I nodded. "Use our office phone. It's not listed anywhere, so it will be almost impossible to track it to our house."

Stella huffed again, then looked at Sy.

"My dearest," he said. "I am in complete agreement with Sid. Not with carrying a gun. But I think a security system is an excellent idea, and using his phone number is an even better one."

"Stella, please?" Sid walked over to her. "For me?"

"Oh, Sid." Stella reached over and held him. "How the hell am I supposed to say no to that?"

Sid's grin took on a slightly evil cast. "You're not." He hugged her back. "I love you, Stella."

"You mean the world to me, too," she said.

It was kind of sad that Stella still couldn't tell Sid that she loved him. But it was part of her dysfunctional background, and there was only so much we could do about that.

January 15 – 16, 1989

The next day, after Sid, Nick, and I got home from mass, Sy called. I picked it up in the breakfast room.

"Stella wants a day to herself," Sy told me. "And I am happy to accommodate her."

"Do you want to come here for the afternoon?" I asked.

"Yes, thank you. I think that would be a most excellent idea."

I debated asking him what he meant, but decided that he'd tell us when he got to the house. When he did, Sid and I got him settled in the library. Nick and Josh had taken the bus to the beach to go skateboarding. I got out my knitting as Sid went off to get the coffee he'd brewed for me and Sy, Bowser puppy following him. Motley sauntered into the room and flopped down next to me. Fritz, a gray tabby, decided to nap on the back of the wingback chair where Sy had settled. Blueberry, a gray, fluffy cat, had sacked out on the walnut baby grand piano's bench.

"Damn it, Bowser!" Sid hollered from the hallway.

"Bowser?" Sy asked.

"The puppy Stella talked us into taking last summer," I said, adjusting a stitch marker. "He keeps getting under Sid's feet."

"Further confirmation that a cat is the most preferable of all animal companions." Sy chuckled as he brushed Fritz's tail from his face.

Bowser trotted into the room. He's a good-sized dog in spite of his short stature - about fifty pounds, with a rough coat, dark on his back and tan underneath, and the head, ears, and stubby legs of a basset hound.

Sid had the coffee mugs on a tray. He served Sy his, then set mine next to me on the lamp table between the two wingback chairs.

"Ahhh," Sy said after a sip from his mug. "Nectar of the gods."

Sid settled onto the piano bench, gently edging Blueberry over. Long John wandered in and made a beeline for Sid's lap.

"It truly is," Sy continued in his usual ponderous fashion. "There are few things more elegant and gracious than a well-made cup of coffee, and few things more rare. Sid, you are a master."

"Thanks, Sy." Sid shifted. "How is Stella doing?"

Sy shook his head. "Sid, my boy, you know perhaps better than any of us just how firmly and deeply Stella holds her convictions. Yesterday was quite the rude awakening, but one she needed. She is dealing with it about as well as one might expect. Nonetheless, it is not easy for her, any more than it was, and is, for you."

Sid frowned. "I can imagine, but..."

"I cannot entirely endorse the way Stella kept her past from you." Sy shifted and took another sip of coffee. "At the same time, I do understand it. I had thought that my family was quite the collection of miserable wretches, and they were. However, the horror of Stella's family eclipsed mine several times over."

"Your family?" I asked.

"I am the youngest of three sons. Coddled from infancy and indulged. It is only now, from the vantage point of old age, that I begin to see and understand my brothers' resentment. They are, alas, gone. As are their wives. I have three nieces and two nephews, but we are not close, largely thanks to my brothers' fears that I would somehow corrupt them." Sy waved his hand. "But as I just now said, what Stella and her sister endured was far, far worse than what I had known."

"Did you know Sheila?" Sid asked.

"Oh, yes." Sy shifted. "I had returned from my studies abroad shortly before you were born, Sid. Stella did not want me to live with her because she was teaching in the public school system, and in those days, she could have gotten fired for living in sin."

"But she gave up that job," I said.

"Yes. However, after it was clear that Sheila was going to remain in residence, I decided that I did not wish to move in with them." Sy winced. "Sheila was extremely manipulative, and for all she could be very, very charming, she was not a pleasant person. And to be honest, I did not fancy living with a small infant."

"I can hardly blame you for that." Sid shrugged.

"Still." Sy shifted in the chair and again brushed Fritz's tail from his face. "I must point out that Stella and I had planned on procreating at one point. Which made your presence, Sid, only a minor deterrent. Sheila was the primary one."

"Stella told me about trying to get pregnant," I said. "She was pretty upset that she couldn't."

"She was devastated." Sy gazed at his mug. "Then Sheila arrived, looking for an abortion. I was quite happy to provide for it. I knew a good doctor, too. But Stella wanted you, Sid. She wanted you desperately. So in deference to Stella's desire, I kept my silence. I will confess to no little surprise that Stella had convinced Sheila to support the three of you. But as time went on, I began to see that it was one odd little mess. I think the term today is dysfunctional. Sheila seemed to hate her sister. She bitterly resented Stella's hold on her, and yet, could not leave her, either."

"Or was it her son?" I asked, then flipped my knitting over to start a new row.

"I highly doubt that." Sy chuckled ruefully. "Stella was completely accurate in her assessment of Sheila's care for you, Sid. You would cry, at two months old, even, and Sheila would become quite enraged, and I saw her slap you more than once. And yet..." Sy winced. "She could also be quite tender with you, especially as you got older. She'd play with you. Admittedly, not often, but she would. And she even volunteered to watch you during the days so that Stella could go back to teaching. Which, quite fortunately, as it turned out, Stella had that fall that Sheila was murdered." Sy squeezed his eyes closed. "I was convinced that Sheila was getting ready to abandon the two of you."

"I wonder why she didn't sooner, if she hated being around me and Stella so much," Sid said.

"She didn't want to be alone," I said.

"I do believe you're right, Lisa," Sy said. He again brushed the cat's tail from his face as he gazed unseeing across the room. "There was one fight in particular. You had to have been around nine months old, Sid. Stella and I had gone to lunch together. Sheila had agreed to watch you. However, when we came back, you had been left alone in your playpen. Two hours later, Sheila returned. Stella was furious and threatened to kick Sheila out. Sheila begged her not to, promising that she would do better, that she would not leave the baby alone." Sy shrugged. "She did again, but not for many months later. You would have thought Sheila had the upper hand, in that Stella was dependent on her for support. Remember, women with infants at home were expected to stay there, not support themselves."

Sid frowned. "Sy, you said just a minute ago that you thought Sheila was getting ready to abandon us. What made you think that? Did you know about Congressman Van Blinn?"

"I did not. But Sheila was growing more confident and cockier around Stella. More likely to directly cross her. And she'd drop hints that she'd found someone who could take care of her better than Stella could. We had no idea that she was considering taking you with her."

Sid's eyebrow lifted. "Do you think Van Blinn could have killed her?"

"I have no idea what to think about that." Sy heaved a deep sigh. "If life with Sheila around had been fraught with annoyances and angst, it was nothing compared to those weeks after she was killed. Stella completely shut down. Utterly numb, and yet, I could tell that she was grieving. But the worst of it was your reaction, Sid. You kept crying for She-She. That's what you called Sheila. She-She. 'Want She-She, want She-She.' It was utterly heart-rending. Stella took it to mean that you knew your true mother was dead and that she was only an inadequate substitute."

"Oh, poor Stella," I gasped.

"Obviously, Sid, you were simply upset by Stella's grieving and that someone you knew was gone." Sy shook his head. "I could not convince Stella of that, however. And yet, after Sheila's death, Stella hung onto you even more tightly. She was terrified that someone would declare her an unfit mother, never mind that she had little choice but to work to support the two of you. Her fears were not eased until the two of you moved to San Francisco a little over a year later."

"Hm." Sid sipped from his mug. "That puts an interesting perspective on things."

"As I hoped it would," said Sy.

Sy stayed for dinner that night, then left after Stella called to thank Sid for providing someplace for Sy to go.

"She thinks that Sundays are going to be the toughest to get used to when it comes to having Sy around full-time," Sid told me as we slid into bed that night. "She really likes having some time to herself once a week."

"I can understand that," I said.

"She's gotten used to having him around during the summers, but now she's got to get used to having him around during the year, too." He snuggled up to me.

"How are you feeling?"

His eyes glittered. "Horny."

"Besides that," I laughed.

Horny is pretty much a chronic state with him. Not that I'm complaining. [You never have. - SEH]

He nuzzled my ear. "Okay, I guess. Sy's perspective is really interesting, and that he witnessed a lot of it adds credence to what Stella has told us. On the other hand, it doesn't shed much light on who killed Sheila, or on our official mission, which is keeping an eye on Van Blinn."

"You're right. And there isn't much we can do about any of it, either." I touched his cheek. "I'm just a little worried about you being messed up by it."

"And I'm glad you are." He gently held my fingers and kissed them. "But we'll get through. We're good that way."

The next morning, I took Nick and Josh to school, then made a pickup. As in met another courier to get something that would either be passed on to someone else, or in this case, was meant for us. Sid was waiting for me when I got back to the house.

"Well?" he asked.

"Looks like a list of the guys that Van Blinn has been looking at," I said, handing him the envelope. "According to Steve and Ray, Van Blinn's looking at these folks because they donated to his campaign last fall, and they don't live in his district or share the same party affiliation."

Sid looked disgusted. "So why would they be trying to get Van Blinn elected unless they want something from him?"

"Exactly. Most of the guys are in New York. We've got two here in Southern California, but that's it."

"Who?"

"Mason Brightman and Earl Manotti. Both are CEOs at different S&Ls."

"Manotti..." Sid's brow creased. "Isn't he that guy with the most trusted banker in L.A. commercial?"

"Oh, him." I scrunched up my face. "I hate that commercial."

"I can't stand him, either." Sid made a face. "He lies like a bleeping rug."

Um. He didn't say bleeping.

"Anyway," Sid continued, pulling his pocket watch from his khaki dress slacks. "I've set up a meeting over at Frank and Esther's in about... forty minutes."

His eyes looked over the jeans and sweater that I was wearing, and he sighed. He was wearing a dark sports coat over a lavender Oxford shirt with a tie - Sid's idea of casual.

"That gives me..." I frowned, ignoring him otherwise. "Shavings. Not nearly enough time. Never mind. We've got to get this taken care of."

I could see Sid biting his tongue. He preferred business wear during work hours. I wanted to be a college professor so that I could wear jeans to work. Okay. There were other, better reasons behind being a college professor.

Part of the issue with my clothes is that I started out as Sid's employee. That made it a lot easier for him to require business wear on weekdays, which wasn't a bad idea. Working at home makes it a lot easier to slack off, and dressing more formally works against that. After we'd become partners in both the writing and side businesses, it was a lot harder for him to carp when I did not feel the same need to Dress for Success. Worse yet, my work ethic was pretty solid no matter what I happened to be wearing, which gave him even less room to complain.

Frank and Esther were waiting for us when we got to their place. Kathy and Jesse arrived within minutes. They settled Keshon into a playpen they'd brought, which did not go over well with Keshon. He immediately began fussing until Sid picked him up and started rocking the eighteen-month-old.

"He doesn't like being on the floor anymore," Kathy said. She's tall, slender, with dark brown skin, and was wearing her hair in tiny braids. "He wants to be up where he can see everything."

"Have we got anything?" I asked.

"It sure would help to know what we're looking for," Esther grumbled.

"Trust us, you don't want to know," I said.

Esther shot me a quick glare. "The car hasn't gone anywhere, except yesterday."

Sid looked at Jesse and Frank, who shrugged.

"He only went to church," Frank said. "That big one out in Anaheim Hills. He didn't stay very long, either."

"What about Saturday?" Sid asked around Keshon's hand.

"Well, the car we have the tracker on didn't go anywhere," Esther said.

I looked at Sid. "I wonder if we should put a tracker on the three other cars there."

"I don't think he's going anywhere," said Jesse. "He's been making a lot of phone calls, which means he hasn't had time to go anywhere. And the times we can confirm that he's not making phone calls, the car has been gone. Usually to that country club up the highway."

"Who's he calling?" Sid asked.

"Mostly his offices in New York and D.C. But he's also been trying to reach an Earl Manotti, who is not returning his calls. The target also called Mason Brightman, and that was very interesting." Jesse shifted. He held up a cassette tape. "Here, let me play that one for you."

We heard the phone ringing from the player next to the monitor, then a secretary announced that he'd reached

Mason Brightman's office. Van Blinn introduced himself and asked to speak to Mr. Brightman. The secretary put him through.

The other phone picked up. "Jimmy! Is that you?"

"Yes, Mason. It's been a while, hasn't it?"

"It has. It has. I see you've come up in the world."

"And you have, too. How many branches does your savings and loan have?"

"Only five." Brightman laughed. "But we're working on expanding. So why are you calling?"

"Eh. Two reasons, actually. Do you remember Sheila from Jane Smith's house?"

Sid and I looked at each other.

"Sheila... Oh, yeah. She was that pretty little Southern kid. A real charmer and a damn good roll in the hay. Wait. She got killed, didn't she?"

"I'm afraid so."

"Yeah, well, it wasn't me." Brightman laughed. "But seriously. They ever catch the jerk that did it?"

"No, they haven't. Some new information has come to light, though. Jane's ledger was found."

"Oh. That could be sticky."

"I wouldn't worry too much. The clients' names are all in some odd code. Even I can't decipher it."

Brightman laughed. "I didn't say I was worried. That was - what? Almost forty years ago."

"Something like that. That doesn't mean Sheila's family has forgotten her."

"She had a family?"

"Yes. They've been located, too. In fact, that's why I'm here in Southern California."

Sid started to curse, then glanced at Keshon and bit back the stream. The others looked at Sid and me, obviously wondering what was going on.

"I'm hoping to work with them to find out what happened to Sheila," Van Blinn continued on the tape.

"That idiot!" Sid snarled.

"Sure," Brightman said. "But there isn't much I can do. I barely remember her, let alone what happened to her."

"Well, maybe you'll think of something. Maybe something one of the other boys said." Van Blinn let out a soft cough. "Oh, and the second reason I wanted to talk to you. I saw your donation to my campaign last fall. It was very generous."

"That's just the kind of guy I am."

"I'm glad. I wouldn't want you to get the impression that your gift will have any effect on how I choose to vote on various issues related to, say, the banking industry."

"You were always a stick in the mud, Jimmy."

"True. But I sleep better at night when I am."

Van Blinn proceeded to tell Brightman where he was staying and gave him the phone number while Sid and I groaned. Keshon fussed a little, and Kathy took him. I could hear Sid cursing Van Blinn out under his breath.

"He's out here investigating a murder?" Esther asked.

"And not just any murder," Frank said, watching both Sid and me.

Jesse chuckled as he began to catch on.

"Wait a minute," said Kathy. "Sid, didn't you tell us at some point that the reason Stella raised you was that your mother had been murdered, and that she'd been a call girl?"

"I must have." Sid shrugged. "And, yes, Sheila was my mother. That's why we're stuck with this stupid case. Because I have a visible reason to be talking to Van Blinn."

"Okay," said Jesse. "Is the case about the bribery attempt or the murder?"

"The bribery attempt," Sid grumbled, and began pacing. "But, yeah, I'm also interested in the murder. Mostly because Stella's hot on the trail. And damn it, she got shot at on Saturday."

"Oh, no!" Kathy gasped.

"We're all fine." Sid looked at Jesse. "You recorded this, when? Friday?"

"Yeah. Eleven-fourteen a.m."

Sid's curse was a hair louder.

"Well, this won't make you feel any better," Kathy said, handing Keshon to Jesse. She pulled some papers from her bag. "I got the campaign finance reports last week. The good news is that they are clear. I was also able to look at the campaign accounts, and they squeak, they're so clean. I haven't been able to get into Van Blinn's personal money, but something about that call makes me think he's behaving himself."

Esther grinned. "I could try to get into his bank's system. Shouldn't be that hard."

Kathy winced a little. Esther wasn't always as concerned as perhaps she should have been about how legal her methods were.

"I am so close to wrapping this one up," Sid said with a sigh. "But if I do, you know that's when Van Blinn is going to do something stupid."

Of course, at that moment, Esther spotted the car moving. I offered to take a turn doing visual surveillance on Van

Blinn, then hurried home to get my blond wig and my ID for my alter ego, Linda Devereaux.

As Sid and I had agreed earlier, if Van Blinn didn't want to meet with me, that made it easier for me to question him as Linda Devereaux. Which might help hide why I was really talking to him. Or maybe he'd find it easier to talk to me. Either way, it just seemed like a good idea.

Thanks to Esther's monitoring system, which had something to do with triangulating satellites, I was able to catch up to Van Blinn at a small diner. He sat in a booth near the back, with a plate glass window behind him, writing away in a black notebook. A plate of pie sat in front of him, and next to a cup of coffee. The counter wound around the dining area, and there was a seat near his table where I could keep an eye on him.

Once I settled in, I heard him chatting pleasantly with the waitress, thanking her for her attention, and no, he didn't need anything else. The waitress slid behind me to her side of the counter and got out her ticket book. I ordered a bacon, lettuce, and tomato sandwich and a cola, figuring I could take that with me if Van Blinn left. It didn't sound like he was going anywhere any too soon, but as soon as you make that kind of assumption, you know what happens.

I was a little bummed that I couldn't get any of my reading done. It would have been just too engrossing, no matter how boring I sometimes found it. So I made notes on what I wanted to cover in the two classes I'd be teaching the next day, then added notes on some things I wanted to look up for Shakespeare's problem plays.

The man who entered the diner next startled me. He was on the small side of average height, slender, with dark hair. He looked very familiar, although I simply could not place him. His eyes swept the diner with the "oh, so casual air that was anything but" of a professional operative. I smiled at him as he looked at me. He smiled politely, but without recognition, then promptly dismissed me when he saw Van Blinn.

Van Blinn saw the newcomer as he approached the table and smiled.

"Noah! What are you doing here?"

Noah slid into the booth as Van Blinn waved the waitress over.

"I called the house where you're staying." Noah's eyes swept the diner again and again, dismissed me. "They said you liked coming here for lunch."

The name tugged at my memory, but I still couldn't place it. The waitress placed my sandwich in front of me, then went to the table.

"Please put Mr. Taplin's order on my check," Van Blinn told the waitress.

The penny dropped. Taplin was regular CIA. I'd run into him on another undercover case around two years before. He'd been rather obnoxious, but then that's how people from the Company tend to be. The Company is what we call the CIA when we're not using ruder terms. I wondered how he knew Van Blinn.

"So what brings you to Southern California?" Van Blinn asked after Taplin had declined to order anything.

"Checking things out." Taplin's voice almost lowered. "They're looking at you."

"That's no surprise." Van Blinn closed his notebook. "Things are going exactly the way I said they would when they passed that bill. Nobody likes hearing I told you so, even if I'm not saying it."

Taplin snorted. "Well, since we're both in town, I came to warn you. Maybe see if I can spot who's doing the surveillance."

I kept my face straight and eyes riveted on my notes. Taplin paid no attention to me. Admittedly, I didn't look like I had when I'd met him. But he should have at least caught the same thing I had when he came in.

"I'm not worried," Van Blinn said. "In fact, one of the reasons I'm here is to make it very clear to certain parties that I have not been bought."

"Which is why they're looking at you."

Van Blinn shrugged. "Then they'll have to keep looking."

Taplin snorted again, then got up, his eyes yet again sweeping the diner, and yet again missing me. He strode from the place. I ordered a piece of apple pie. Van Blinn finally ate his, then left. It was good pie. I finished mine, then called Esther to get Van Blinn's location - he was headed back to Wanzyck's place. I followed him as far as the outside of the complex. I pulled around to the part of the street overlooking the back of the house, and stopped my truck just long enough to look through my binoculars at the sliding glass door to Van Blinn's room. Van Blinn went in, settled in front of the television, and picked up the phone.

I took off, keeping an eye out for Taplin or anyone else.

January 17 - 18, 1989

(Sid's Voice)

I will concede that I was definitely not happy to hear that Noah Taplin was sniffing around. Nor was I sure what to make of Lisa's assessment of his skills. As annoying as those Company fucks were, they weren't generally stupid. Petty, vindictive, obtuse as hell, but not stupid.

The one thing that seemed pretty clear was that Van Blinn was being unfairly targeted for political purposes. Lisa and I agreed that we were done, and I called the rest of the team to let them know that we had what we needed and were ending operations. We couldn't do much about the tracker on the car, but Esther disabled it. Jesse took the van out to Newport Beach and got the tap off the phone. The only reason we held off on filing the report was that Lisa didn't want to get Lillian in trouble in case somebody got a bug up their ass about us ending things so early.

Then we tried to figure out what to do about Van Blinn and Sheila's death. I decided to take the lead on that.

That next morning, I caught Hannah Davis in, and she agreed to speak with me around one that afternoon.

Her house was in the Hollywood Hills, on a steep, turning road, and half built into a hillside. She'd clearly lived there for a very long time, with an old brass front doorbell and doorknob that had tarnished at uneven rates. The paint job looked faded, but was not chipped, and the walls were stuccoed with dark wood shutters.

Davis opened the door and let me into the spacious living room. The huge Persian rug was faded, yet dark wood floors gleamed around it. A large brown velvet corner group sofa looked out over sliding glass doors leading to a faded wood deck, strewn with white patio furniture and plants in hanging pots and stands. Shelves lined the walls, some glass-fronted, others not. They were filled with books and the many mementos of a very long career.

That felt a little odd. Davis couldn't have been much more than ten years older than me. But then I remembered, she'd been acting since she was eleven or twelve.

She wasn't hiding her age, either. She had delicate laugh lines around her eyes and mouth. Silver threads were scattered through her blond hair that had been cut in a wedge. Her figure was actor thin, and she wore jeans and a full sweater over them.

"Come on in and have a seat," she said. "Can I get you anything? Some Perrier?"

"That sounds good. Thanks."

She reappeared a moment later with two glasses filled with ice and the bubbling water, ornamented with a lime slice.

"I know this might be difficult for you," I began slowly.

"You mean about what Mom did for a living?" She laughed ruefully. "I couldn't care less about that. There may have been some studio heads who would have had a conniption if they'd known way back when." She sudden-ly sniffed. "No. It's just that a friend of mine passed away last week, and between helping his boyfriend clear out the home care junk and grieve and all that, I've been missing Mom more than usual. It's only been a couple years since she died. Would you please tell your aunt that I meant to call her back?"

"Sure." I sipped and waited.

"She was a wonderful mom. I know that sounds pretty weird, having started out in a brothel. But Mom kept me insulated from the worst of it." Her eyes pierced me. "I don't know how much you know about the life."

"I, eh..." Oh, that was uncomfortable. "I've bought it before. I didn't do it often. I used to be into sleeping around, and sometimes I'd need a quick connection. It seemed like just another way to have sex, and the most efficient way." I winced. "Until my wife caught me once."

"Oh?" Grinning, her eyebrows rose.

"She wasn't my wife then. But, shit, she gave me hell." I shrugged. "I haven't bought it since. Haven't needed to."

"Most guys who buy it don't need to." Davis took a sip of her water. "I remember reading that once, and asked Mom about it. She said that sounded right to her. All of her clients could have found girlfriends, and most of them were married."

"How well did you know her clients?"

Davis shook her head. "I didn't. Like I said, I was very insulated from that part of it. I remember when five-thirty, six rolled around, Mom would take me up to our little set of rooms and have me lock the door. I think most of those guys would have been shocked to find out that Mom even had a kid. She let me hang around the girls, though." Davis laughed again. "She later told me it was the best way she could think of to keep me from turning tricks."

"Sounds like she had quite a sense of humor."

"Oh, yeah." Tears filled her eyes. "She needed it. Women do not get into that business for the fun of it. Oh, I know some say that they like their work, but I really think that's what they tell themselves. I once asked Mom why she got into it. She just said that she didn't have a choice." Davis frowned. "I think it was something about my father, but I don't know. She wouldn't say and didn't even put his name on my birth certificate."

"Maybe she didn't know who he was," I said. "Sheila didn't know who fathered me. It says unknown on my birth certificate."

"Mom knew who my father was. I got that much. She just refused to say any more."

"How well did you know Sheila?"

"Oh, I hung out with them before the clients arrived. Tina. Clare, MaryAnn, Lynn, Miranda, Earline, and Rhoda. And Sheila. They were okay. Sheila was a little weird in that she'd like me one minute, then not want me around another. Earline, though. Oh, my god. She gave me the creeps. I remember when I was around fifteen - I was still going to the studio school then. But I had to read this short story called The Bad Seed. You know? About that little girl who kills people? I hated that story, mostly because it reminded me of Earline. She could be really, really cold and calculating. But, if I'm honest, all of them were in many ways. They were hard women."

"What about the night that Sheila died?"

"I don't remember much about it." Davis shook her head again, then sipped. "There was a lot of screaming, then Mom came up to the room and said that something terrible had happened and that Sheila was dead. I don't know why, but she was very, very scared. Kept saying we were getting out of there. A week or two later, we're on a train to California and Hollywood. I think it was something to do with one of the clients. She wouldn't talk much about them, either. She'd sometimes make a snide comment about some guy who reminded her of so-and-so. But that was it. And she really clammed up when it came to my father or the night Sheila died." She took another sip of her water, then looked at me. "How much did your aunt tell you about your mother?"

"Next to nothing," I said. "I didn't find out she was a prostitute and that she was murdered until two and a half years ago. Stella just carried all that inside her. All her bitterness because the cops never did that much to find the man who killed her sister."

Davis groaned loudly. "What is it with them? Like, hearing about the bad stuff is automatically going to corrupt us?"

I had to laugh. "Stella said she didn't want to pass all that crap onto me. I can sort of see that, but shit, it drives me nuts." I got up. "Anyway, thank you very much for talking to me."

"You're very welcome." She got up, too. "It's good to talk about Mom."

I left, then almost groaned when I got back to my car. It was getting awfully close to three when Alicia Mendoza would arrive for her two hours of lessons. I made it, but just barely, and it was really good having to focus on teaching her how to count beats. Alicia was (and still is) incredibly intuitive about her music. She taught herself to play piano by listening to what she heard on the radio. So she'd learned to feel her way around a piece. The problem was that if she was going to have a concert career, she was going to have to read music.

We did get a bit of a breakthrough that day, which helped my mood a lot. Also, with Alonzo Carrera coming in for the final hour right after Alicia, I did not get a chance to talk to Stella about Davis until after six.

We were cleaning up when Stella started in on me.

"Well? Did you talk to anybody today?"

"I talked to Hannah Davis, the madam's daughter," I said, sorting through several sheet music books.

"And…?"

I went over what Davis had told me. Stella snorted.

"What kind of mother raises her child in a brothel?"

"One who doesn't feel she has another choice," I said calmly. "There are plenty of people who would ask the same thing about a mother who let her kid run around buck naked all the time and screwing everything female within reach."

"That's normal and natural!" Stella gaped at me in horror.

"And damned unconventional." I held up my hands. "I'm fine with it, by the way. I don't think I turned out badly. But it does mean we can't judge how other parents make their choices. Right?"

"I suppose not," Stella said.

Later, after Lisa and I and the boys had eaten dinner and Darby and Nick had been sent to the library to finish their homework, I told Lisa about Hannah Davis. She sighed.

"That's all very interesting, but it doesn't tell us very much," she said.

She sat in her desk chair, two books in front of her.

"I know." I paced the room. "I don't know what to think about it."

"Neither do I." Her face got that pained look. "In fact, I don't know what to think about anything. I'm sorry, darling, but I'm just so peeved at the way that stupid surveillance case put me behind on my reading, that's all I can think about." She shook her head as if to clear it. "Anyway, I'd better get back on this. Do you mind?"

I smiled at her, my heart filling. "No. I appreciate the way you put it aside to watch Van Blinn for us."

She grabbed her two books, and I followed her into the library. She settled herself on one of the two dark green wingback chairs and arranged the tan leather hassock, and put her feet up. The boys sat together on the window seat with two wooden tray tables and their homework in front of them. They were squabbling over something, as usual. I had stopped hearing it months before. I found the book I was reading on the lamp table between the two chairs. I would have played piano - we had a walnut baby grand in there. But it distracted Darby, who did not need distractions when it came to his homework.

At nine o'clock, I sent the boys to bed.

"Do you mind if I work on some Mozart?" I asked, setting my book down.

"No. Go ahead." Her eyes stayed on what she was reading.

"I'll play softly."

I was working my way through Mozart's piano sonatas and had gotten to the eighth one. I started with the allegro, but kept it quiet. When I'd worked through it a couple of times, and started the andante cantabile, I heard soft whistling and snorting.

I looked over at the wingback chair. Lisa's head had rolled back, her eyes were closed, and her cute little whistling snore was going full force. My poor darling worked so hard. People don't realize how much energy and time are involved in teaching. Plus, there was all the work she was doing for her PhD program. She was essentially working one and a half full-time jobs even without Quick-line.

I got up from the keyboard. It was close enough to ten p.m. as it was. I got her awake enough to come up to bed and make love. She'll always wake up long enough for that.

(Lisa's Voice)

It was one of those things that happened. Just when we'd thought we'd wrapped something up, we'd find out we weren't done. That morning, while we were eating break-fast, Sid and I got paged.

Sid drove the boys to school, and I called Lillian, who had paged us.

"This just gets more annoying," she told me when we'd confirmed our codes. "Clint Foster says that somebody on his side talked to Van Blinn's office and found out that Van Blinn has been talking to campaign donors."

Clint Foster is our liaison with the Company.

"Yeah," I said. "We heard him talk to one of them. Van Blinn said that he wanted to make the donor absolutely sure that the donation wasn't going to affect how he vot-ed."

"That's good to know." She grumbled something else. "Alright. We'd better find out where else Clint's crew has been sniffing around."

"Fair enough," I sighed. "Did Clint say who on his side was doing the checking?"

"Why do you ask?"

"I may have run across one of them yesterday." I bit my lip. "The interesting thing is that Van Blinn knew him and told him the same thing - that he can't be bought by the campaign donations."

Lillian cursed. "Did this other operative see you?"

"Yes and no," I said. "He saw me, but didn't look like he'd made me as surveillance and even said that he was trying to see who was."

Lillian cursed even more strongly. "If you're talking about who I think you're talking about, he holds quite a bit of influence over people who should, quite frankly, know better. But Taplin knows his politics."

"Taplin. That was him."

"He should have been dead years ago. Why he isn't, no one knows. But if Noah Taplin is involved, then you'll have to find out who else Taplin is talking to."

"Okay." I bit my lip. "Dare I ask who Taplin is, besides Division One?"

Division One was our code for the main part of the CIA.

"He's mostly a desk jockey." Lillian's voice dripped with disdain. "I've had a feeling for years that he's got somebody by the short hairs. They pulled him out of the field in the early seventies because he screwed up an operation and got one of our best people killed. Marge Bowers broke his jaw some years ago after he exposed her entire network by talking about it on an unsecured phone line. She said he was lucky she didn't have her sidearm on her, or she would have killed him. She got the usual reprimand and Taplin got off, then later promoted as an attaché to various congressmen, supposedly for security purposes."

"Is that when you began to suspect that he had the goods on somebody?"

"The reprimand was the usual sexism." Lillian snorted. "You have no idea, my dear, just how bad it was for us women in intelligence. We were getting some of the best intel, but not only did we not get credit for it, the men gave us hell. It was even worse in the Bureau. It's getting better, but you still have a lot of guys who were around during J. Edgar's reign, and you can imagine what that was like. That's why you find a lot more women in the shadow agencies. The higher ups could get the benefit of the work we did without having to give us credit for it. Nor did they have to deal with us that much."

"Wow." My brow creased. "But I'm confused. Van Blinn made it clear that his donors were not going to get what they wanted, and Taplin heard that as well as I did."

"Yes, but the odds are decent that Taplin is the one setting Van Blinn up. Only one more reason why we hate these kinds of jobs and why we need to find out who else he's talking to. But don't attempt surveillance on Taplin. Just talk to the other campaign donors, and do it as Linda Devereaux."

"But Taplin knows that name from the Kansas case."

Lillian chuckled. "Exactly. If we have to risk burning one of your alter egos, I'd rather burn that one. Besides, it might just scare Taplin off if he realizes that we're also looking at him."

I went ahead and made a few calls while Sid was still out dropping the boys off at school. He was not happy when he got home.

"I'm sorry you have to deal with it, lover," he said, watching me pace in the office. "On the other hand, Brightman does sound like a good suspect for Sheila's murder."

"There is that." I grimaced. "Given how nasty he sounded on that phone tap Jesse got, it's probably just as well that I'm going in with my alter ego."

Sid had to leave shortly after that to talk to Tina Goetz and Paul West, whose phone number I'd found for him. I changed into a nice wool skirt and blazer, with a silk blouse underneath, then packed my makeup and blond wig in my bag.

I went first to the library to look up Mason Brightman in all the different local directories. But I found him in the Who's Who. You can imagine my surprise (as in none whatsoever) that he was the owner and CEO of a decent-sized savings and loan. I also looked up Earl Manotti and found the main branch of his chain of S&Ls.

I spoke to Manotti from a nearby diner's payphone, introducing myself as a freelance writer doing a story on political donations. Manotti told me that Mason Brightman had talked him into donating to Van Blinn's campaign. However, Manotti had not talked to Van Blinn. After I mentioned that I might have a Mr. Taplin competing with me, Manotti said that he hadn't heard from anyone else.

Brightman, on the other hand, wanted to talk to me at his office. So after lunch, I piled on the makeup in the diner's restroom, put on my wig, and headed over to the office in Glendale. It was in a high-rise on Brand Avenue.

Getting parked was no small trick, but once I got upstairs, I found the right office and was ushered into Brightman's space almost immediately.

It was a corner office, with windows overlooking the foothills to the north and the boulevard below. Brightman was fairly short and somewhat rounded, balding, and wore half glasses on the end of his nose. Everything about him and his office screamed money and power, and his smile had a smarmy edge to it, as if I should be prostrate with gratitude that I'd been allowed into his inner sanctum.

The first few questions were strictly about campaign finances. I'd explained that I'd heard about him because he'd donated to Congressman Van Blinn's campaign.

"What happens if the politician you're donating to votes against things you want?" I asked.

Brightman sniggered. "Listen, sweetheart, they always do what I want. Guys like me can run those wimps out of office in a New York second."

"I heard you used to know Congressman Van Blinn some time ago."

"Yeah. That's how I knew to donate to his campaign."

"Were you friends?"

"Friends enough. We shared the same, uh, recreational facility, you might say." Brightman adjusted the vest of his exquisitely tailored suit. "In fact, that's how I know he's going to go along with me and my buddies. I might have something on him. A lot of years ago, one of the girls at the, um, facility got murdered. Jimmy was real sweet on her. He probably didn't kill her, but it wouldn't look too good if I let it get out to his constituents that he did."

"But aren't you worried about it backfiring and getting you in trouble?"

"Why?" He sniggered again. "I'm not doing anything illegal. Let me tell you. Jimmy Van Blinn had better watch his ass around me."

"I can imagine." I looked down at my notes. "There may be another reporter, a Mr. Taplin, writing a competing piece on this."

Brightman laughed out loud. "Sweetheart, if you think he's a reporter, you'd better watch your own ass."

"He's not? Have you talked to him?"

"All the time." Brightman sniggered again. "How do you think I got the goods on Jimmy Van Blinn?"

"Well." I got up and put my notepad back in my purse. "I think I've got everything I need."

"You'll let me see that article before it runs, right?"

"We'll see."

Brightman's smile grew menacing. "You'll let me see it. Because, see? I can hurt you. And if you say I threatened you? No one will believe that. Trust me, doll, I've hurt sweet young things like you before and no one ever knew."

"Interesting that you believe that," I said, utterly fed up and drawing myself up to my full height. "Because you only think you can hurt me. If you try, you're going to find out that any muscle you hire isn't as good as you thought. And I will hurt you back and let everyone know that you got worked over by this sweet young thing."

I turned and left the office feeling like I sorely needed a shower.

January 18 – 19, 1989

(Sid's Voice)

My first stop that morning was to see Tina Goetz. She was a widow living in San Marino, in a huge white Colonial house with a circular driveway. Goetz was her married name. Her maid opened the door and led me to the huge living room, decked out in Eighteenth Century splendor, with blue satin upholstery on the white and gilt curlicued chairs and sofa. The furniture was grouped around a large matching coffee table bearing a huge arrangement of fresh flowers. Everything was arranged to stunning effect in front of a massive white stone fireplace. About the only thing missing were portraits of long-dead ancestors on the walls.

Goetz came in wearing a simple yellow shirtwaist dress with a full skirt, single pearl earrings, and a pearl necklace. The funny thing was, even though she had the retro, matronly fifties thing going on, an easy sensuality wafted off of her. I couldn't help but be attracted by it. Good thing for me, Lisa was (and still is) even sexier.

"Oh, my god, you look like Sheila," she said, her voice smooth, but with a heavy New York accent.

I smiled and shrugged. "I know."

"Well, sit down. What would you like? I've got wine, liquor."

"I'm fine, thanks." I settled onto the couch.

She smoothed her skirt under her as she sat in one of the chairs and crossed her ankles.

"Miranda told me that someone had found Jane's ledger," she said. "Was that you?"

"Uh, no. But that's why I'm here. We're hoping to find out what happened to Sheila."

Goetz rolled her eyes. "Look. I would not have wished what happened to her on anybody, even her. But I gotta be honest. She was not the nicest person you've ever met. I felt horrible about her getting it, but I wasn't surprised."

"Why?"

Goetz winced. "I know she was your mother."

"Her sister, Stella, was my mother," I said. "I never knew Sheila."

"Huh. That makes sense." Goetz shrugged. "So. Well, Sheila was really selfish. Okay. We all could be. But Miranda and MaryAnn, they'd lend you make up or a dress. Sheila and a couple of the others? It didn't matter if your best client was coming in five minutes and you just found a stain on your nightgown. They wouldn't do squat. But if they needed something, they'd bend over backwards to convince you that they had a right to something you had. And, sweetheart, given what we did, you can bet we knew how to bend." She snorted as I chuckled. "The worst of it was, Sheila had the nicest room in the house. She'd even got to pick her own wallpaper. We all wanted her room. You'd think she could afford to be a little more generous, but not her."

I nodded. "Do you remember the night Sheila was killed?"

"It wasn't that night. I mean, it had to have been late in the afternoon, early evening. Some of the blood had dried, you know? And I found her at seven-thirty."

"You found her?"

"Oh, yeah. Believe me, nothing worse than finding a stiff. Especially one that's somebody you knew."

As many stiffs as I've turned up, I had to agree with her.

"What happened?" I asked.

"Jane asked me to go up and see why Sheila wasn't responding to her call. That weenie, Jimmy Van Blinn, was in the waiting room, asking to see her."

"Could he have killed her?"

Goetz shrugged. "Could have. Who knows? But it scared the shit out of Jane. Look. Most of us were used to getting knocked around sometimes by the clients. Jane was pretty good about booting the guys that hit. Assuming we told her. Hey, it was income, right? But this was nasty. I don't really know why. When Jane ran for Hollywood, I thought why the fuck am I here? So I ran for Hollywood, too. Found the first guy with money I could find and got him to marry me. And here I am."

"And in a very nice place, indeed." I smiled at her. "How long have you been widowed?"

Her face creased. "Let's not talk about that."

"Okay. I'm told Sheila was pretty popular with the clients. Anyone who was particularly focused on her?"

She glared at me. "How fucking stupid do you think I am? I do not know who killed Sheila. But even if I did, do you think I'd tell anybody else? Not while that fuck is still out there. I like staying alive, thank you."

"I understand," I said, putting my hands up. "It's just my aunt. She wants to know what happened to her sister."

Goetz rolled her eyes, then sighed. "Okay. I gotta give you that. But, see? I really don't know. And that's the scary part. I don't know. I say the wrong thing and my goose is cooked. You know what I mean?"

"I know exactly what you mean." I sighed. "I'm a little worried about that, myself. The problem is, my aunt has been carrying this around for over thirty years. Not knowing, pissed to hell because the cops didn't do shit about it. I have to try to find out."

"I understand." Goetz also sighed. "But, really? It was no surprise. Sheila was one brass plated bitch. You know what I mean?" Goetz looked at me, obviously thinking something over. "Look. I'll be honest. I really do not know what happened to Sheila. I feel bad that she died. It's what got me looking for a rich man to marry. But I do not know who killed her."

"Well, thank you for sharing what you do know," I said, getting up.

We did the usual goodbyes and I left. I wasn't sure what to make of that interview. When someone is working as hard as Goetz was to make herself look honest, you have to believe that they're lying through their teeth. The question is about what? That Goetz was worried about the real perp I could believe. The rest of it, not so much.

I got in my Beemer and flipped on the radio. Getting around L.A. at that time usually meant depending on traffic reports from the local radio stations. I'd just missed the one report on my favorite news station and was already on the freeway through downtown Los Angeles on the way to Brentwood, on the west side, when the next one came on with a Sigalert on Interstate 10 westbound. In other words, a crash causing at least one lane to be closed.

I went to the surface streets, but both Pico and Olympic were jammed with traffic from the freeway. I called West's office on my cell phone to let him know I was going to be late for our lunch meeting, and went up to Santa Monica Boulevard.

Traffic being the ongoing grief that it is, West seemed pretty sympathetic when I got to his office. He was tall and kind of scrawny, with glasses. I got the impression from the way his shoulders slumped under his expensive suit, that he'd been picked on as a kid. Which partly explained why he was so eager to show me how well he was doing.

The office was plush, I'll give him that. It was on the fifth floor over San Vicente Boulevard at Bundy, and featured thick carpet, an elegant reception area with some good art on the walls and professionally arranged fresh flowers in a crystal dish on the credenza next to the door.

West had me escorted to his office, which was lined with books and overlooked San Vicente. His wood desk was modern and perfectly neat, with the deskpad, phone and computer arranged at perfect 90-degree angles.

"What do you think?" he asked, smiling proudly.

"Very nice," I said.

"We've got a full computer system with state of the art software," he said. "Plus I've got six attorneys working for me, nine accountants, and a whole crew of clerks, para-legals and bookkeepers. We're one of the biggest firms in Los Angeles. Our clients average six and seven-figure an-nual incomes, and new clients typically see a sixty-percent reduction in their tax burden."

"Good for you," I said.

Okay. Lisa's and my money from Quickline was not even close to being the larger part of our income. But we were, technically, government employees, and that does have an impact on how you look at paying taxes. What West called a tax burden was the money I got for risking my neck to keep him and his clients safe. But even if I had been able to tell him about my top-secret job, it was not the sort of thing that would have registered with him. I pasted the usual smile on my face and followed him to the office dining room.

"How do you like your steak?" West asked me as he showed me the real cherry wood dining table, laid with good silver and crystal wine glasses.

I hesitated. "Uh, medium. Thanks."

The steak was very good, and served alongside some nicely scalloped potatoes and asparagus. I accepted the glass of Chateau Petrus, trying to think of how I was going to bring up West's relationship with Sheila when he brought up the subject himself.

"You know. I'd heard some rumors that Sheila was pregnant, back in forty-nine," West said around a bite of very rare meat. He looked at me. "That's when I first knew her. At University of Miami. She was my first time, you know. That was in forty-six. I was a senior by the time she left Florida. We had her for a frat party, and that was the last time I saw her before I went to New York."

There's a reason I rarely eat red meat. It was bad enough that the steak was landing in my stomach like so many bricks. But the turn I got as West chuckled, then attacked the potatoes...

"Hey. You look like you're the right age." He grinned. "I could be your daddy."

My entire gut screamed no, but I held onto my cool and smiled again.

"We'll never know," I said. "But I'm told you also knew Sheila in New York."

"Yeah. Went up there after law school and got on with a major firm. I was kinda hoping to see Sheila, and did a few times. Then I got a great offer to come out here in… Sixty-four. The wife was tired of the snow. We both grew up in Florida." He grinned again. "Hey. I know a very nice house not far from here, if you want a little entertainment after lunch."

"Uh, no thanks. Do you remember the night Sheila died?"

"God, yes." He shuddered. "Don't know what happened because we guys were all shut out. Couldn't get shit. Jane told us it was to keep us safe from the cops, but come on. We were in New York. Like they gave a fuck? Then, when Jane split two weeks later, I figured something big was up."

"Any guesses as to who might have killed Sheila?"

"Jimmy Blinn?" West shrugged. "Mason Brightman might have. He could get rough with the girls. You know, he's out here now. CEO of one of the biggest S&Ls in Southern California. And owner, too, I think."

"Have you had much contact with either of them since then?"

"Nah. Been too busy saving my clients money." He grinned again. "And speaking of…"

"I'm fine with my representation," I said quickly.

"You look like you're pulling in some serious cash. I'm sure I could help you out with what you're forking over to the government."

My smile grew strained. "I'm fine with my representation. In fact, I'd better get to my next appointment. Thank you for lunch."

I got out of there as fast as I could.

(Lisa's Voice)

Poor Sid was not in good shape when he got home that afternoon. He does not eat a lot of red meat, and it can upset his stomach.

"I don't think it's just the steak," he said as I gave him the Tums bottle.

He put down the photo of Sheila that he'd been looking at to twist the top off and shake a couple of the antacids into his hand.

"I'm sure the steak isn't," I said, settling into my desk chair. I'd already washed the makeup off my face, but was still wearing the skirt, blouse, and jacket. "I mean, it's bad enough, but thinking that jackass might be my sire would be enough to make me nauseous."

Sid chuckled, then shuddered. "The funny thing is, I don't get why I'm feeling that way about Paul West, specifically. Admittedly, I've never identified with guys like that. But they've never given me the creeps before. Van Blinn does the same thing to me."

"Maybe it's me," I said. "Like those guys who run their wives down all the time. That didn't bother you until you had a wife."

"Oh, it bothered me before we got married." He frowned. "It was one of the reasons I thought marriage was such a crock. I just didn't think about it that much. It was what guys do. They act like assholes, and I got more sex than any of them because I didn't. It wasn't until we got married that I started thinking about how that behavior affected you. All the trouble you have seeing yourself as the incredibly sexy woman you are, and those guys back in Kansas were talking about you in the crudest terms. And suddenly I get it. If that's what being sexy is to other guys, I wouldn't want to see myself as sexy, either."

"And now, you've got these powerful men expecting you to think the way they do." I smiled softly at him.

"I've been dealing with assholes like that my entire adult life. I have no idea why it's bugging me now. Wait." Sid cocked his head as he looked at the photo of Sheila. "I think I know what it is. It's the connection to prostitution. I mean it, Lisa. All my life, buying sex on occasion was just another way of getting it. It never occurred to me that prostitution isn't about sex. That it's about power. It's why I never got off on S and M. That's all about power, and that isn't sex to me. But West wanted to show off how rich and powerful he is by offering to take me for some fun and games as part of his big pitch for his practice."

"And he could also be the unwitting sperm donor that resulted in you being here." I smiled as Sid gagged. "Van Blinn was all set to be your step daddy. I don't think it's just that our values are so different from theirs or the fact that they so blithely assume that you share those values. It's like you just said. You're also now thinking about how those values affect others like me and Stella."

"And Janey and Ellen," Sid sighed.

"And the woman who gave birth to you and who was probably killed because of those values."

His gaze fell on the photo again. "That's it exactly." He blinked, then looked over at me. "Now what?"

I grinned. "Let me tell you about the not very charming jackass that I dealt with today."

So I did. There were not many conclusions to be made, although Sid laughed when I told him about Brightman trying to threaten me.

"You only look harmless, my darling," he chuckled, pulling me into his arms.

Nick and Darby arrived home just then. We ate dinner early, then Sid hurried to choir practice. He plays the organ for the choir at church.

The next day, between being worried that I was getting more and more behind on my reading, and having a lecture to attend, then classes to teach, I did not think about Van Blinn, or Taplin, or anything except school. Which did not put me in a good mood that afternoon after my second section of Basic Composition.

Maggie stayed after class, and she was not happy.

"Am I ever going to get an A from you?" she snarled.

"You've got two typos in that paragraph," I pointed out.

"So my fingers slipped."

"That's the point of this class. To help you make sure your fingers don't slip. They won't let you get away with that excuse in the business world."

Maggie huffed. "Why do you have to be so mean?"

"I'm not being mean," I said, holding onto my patience with both hands. "I'm making you work."

"Oh. So you think I'm stupid after all."

"No," I growled. "The exact opposite. Your spelling scores are better than most of the class. And the only person I know who understands logical flow better than you do is Sid."

"But you grade me harder than anybody else."

I sighed and blushed a little. "Possibly. Probably."

"That's not fair!"

"Why?" My dander was up and then some. "Because I expect you to work for your grades? Because I want you to be your best? Because I know darned well you can handle it? For Heaven's sakes, Maggie. You don't want me to let you slide. Letting you slide is what says I think you're stupid. Not making you work. You want a good grade, then, dammit, earn it!"

Maggie gasped, then strode from the room as I deflated. It was so frustrating.

I come by my smarts honestly, as does Mae, who is even smarter than I am. Both Mama's and Daddy's families are very intelligent people. But what makes my aunts, uncles, and cousins so incredibly aggravating is that they have a deep suspicion of anyone who has more education than they do. Which includes anybody who went past high school. Like poor Maggie, who had been told all her life that her looks would get her by, that she didn't need an education, and was too stupid to get one, anyway.

I groaned. Fortunately, my darling son, who loves education and finding things out and all that, appeared in the doorway to the room, and we went off to my truck. We were having so much fun talking over our days and what we were learning that I didn't put on the radio and the traffic report.

Which is why I was blindsided when I got home to Sid's solemn face. Nick's eyebrows rose, and his face grew anxious. No surprise. Nick spends a lot of time worrying about us.

"What's going on?" I asked, my own heart beating hard.

"I just heard it on the news coming home," Sid said. "They found Van Blinn dead today."

I gaped. "What? Did he have a heart attack or something?"

Sid shook his head. "An apparent homicide."

"Where's Darby?" I asked.

"In the library, doing homework for a change." Sid nodded at Nick. "It's okay, Nick."

"But it's something you're working on," Nick groaned.

Sid pulled Nick into his arms. "Yeah, it is. But you know we can't talk about it. Why don't you go help Darby before dinner?"

"Sure." Nick slid away.

"Did you call Lillian?" I asked.

As if in answer, my pager, and presumably Sid's, went off. It was Lillian. Sid called her, but didn't have any more to tell her than he'd just told me. I was not surprised that Lillian wanted us to find out what we could.

January 20, 1989

T he next morning found me piling more makeup on my face and putting on my blond wig. Special Agent Linda Devereaux was going to Newport Beach to get what I could on the murder of Congressman James Van Blinn in the bedroom where he'd been staying with friends.

I started with the Newport Beach Police Department, where I flashed my ID at the front desk. That normally would have gotten me escorted back to the detectives' room and introduced to the detectives in charge of the case. Instead, a portly man in a dark polyester suit came out to the front foyer.

"ID?" he demanded.

"And you are?" I showed the ID to him. "I'm trying to get information on the Van Blinn case."

The detective sniffled. "Lieutenant Lee Perrick. No can do on Van Blinn."

"What do you mean?"

"I can't give you any information. Can't show you the files. Can't share squat."

My eyes opened wide. "Why not?"

"Orders came down from the top. No sharing with anyone." He shifted his feet, then looked me up and down. "What's your interest?"

"The vic was a congressman." I swallowed, suddenly thinking that wouldn't be enough for a regular FBI agent to intervene. "And there's an issue of national security. It's top secret."

"That's my problem," he said, glaring at me. "It's top secret."

"I have the clearance and the Need to Know. Code—"

His hand went up. "Spare me. I don't care what fancy code you're spouting. I have orders. No sharing. Period."

"Where's your supervisor?" My dander was back up and running.

"I am the supervisor." He snarled, then backed off and sighed. "Look, honey, I don't want to be a pain in the ass. But I've got orders."

"Right," I said, even as I bristled at being called honey. "You can't violate that. I'll see what I can do on my end."

I left the station firmly convinced that if another fat old man called me sweetheart or honey, I was going to pound him into meatballs. The fact that I was (and am) perfectly capable of doing so did not help.

I left the station and drove toward the Wanzyck residence and to the road around back. Sure enough, there was yellow crime scene tape across the sliding glass door to Van Blinn's room. The screen door had been set aside on the back wall of the house. I pulled a pair of binoculars from under the passenger seat of my truck. Yes, the sliding glass door was off its track, although it had been put almost back in place.

I stashed the binoculars, then drove around to the complex gate. Flashing my FBI ID got me in without any questions, and I drove straight to the Wanzyck house. The Hispanic maid had me wait while she talked to someone inside, then let me in. She was a small woman, slightly rounded with coal black hair and a timid mien.

Now, I am not (I hope) one of those people who believe that members of the clergy should live in poverty. If Wanzyck's flock believed that he was worth what it cost to decorate and maintain the house he lived in, well, more power to them. But it was awfully ostentatious. The worst of it was, I was trying so hard not to judge him for it because I hate that kind of judgmentalism. And feeling guilty because I was judging him.

Wanzyck stood as I entered the cavernous living room.

"Hello. You are?" he asked.

"Special Agent Linda Devereaux," I said, showing him my ID case. "FBI. I'm here trying to find out what happened to Congressman Van Blinn."

"Oh." He blinked, confused. "Well. It's been very upsetting. Mrs. Wanzyck and I had just gotten in yesterday morning. We'd been on a retreat in Hawaii. My mother-in-law had stayed here to keep the congressman company. He... He was her guest."

My eyebrows rose. "You weren't concerned about any impropriety?"

"No." Wanzyck laughed. "The congressman... Eh, he was not going to be doing much. He'd promised he wouldn't, as well. And my mother-in-law, well, the maid sleeps in the room with her. In case she wakes up and needs something."

"I see." All too well, actually. "Is your mother-in-law available?"

"I'm afraid not." Wanzyck looked a little anxious as he looked back into the house. "She's resting. She was very upset. As was Mrs. Wanzyck. My wife found the congressman, you know. Her mother had told her that she hadn't seen him that morning, and my wife went to check on him." Wanzyck shuddered. "Very upsetting."

"I understand." Given that I have a phobia of corpses, I did. I sighed. "I suppose I can talk to them later. Can I see the room?"

"Oh, no. No." Wanzyck swallowed. "Lieutenant Perrick was very clear. It's not been released yet. No one is to go in without his specific approval. We can't even go in and clean. The police have already removed all of the congressman's personal belongings. Lieutenant Perrick said that he'd see to getting them to the congressman's family."

"I see." I pressed my lips together, wondering why the heck Perrick was keeping such a tight lid on the case.

That Van Blinn had been a member of Congress probably had something to do with it. But that only made it more likely that Perrick would cooperate with a federal agent.

"Have the police given you any details about what happened?" I asked. "I'd like to verify a few things."

"Not much," said Wanzyck. "Just that someone had broken into the room. It looked like he'd been smothered. Mrs. Wanzyck said that she didn't see any blood in the room, and if his tongue hadn't been sticking out, she would have thought he'd died of a heart attack."

"Didn't your house's alarm go off?"

Wanzyck shrugged. "It did. But my mother-in-law told the security people and the police that it was a false alarm. They saw no reason to question it and left."

"Well." I thought for a moment. "I appreciate you telling me this. I'll call you if I have any more questions."

As I turned to go, he put his hand on my arm. "Agent Devereaux, have you been saved?"

"Yeah." I pulled my arm away.

"Where do you go to church?" His eyes lit up.

"That's my business," I said, getting really annoyed.

It's why I tell Sid to just lie about his beliefs with these guys. There isn't a hope in Hades that you're going to get through to them.

Wanzyck looked at me sadly. "I only ask because it's the kind thing to do."

"As in it wouldn't be very nice if I went to hell because you didn't say anything." I rolled my eyes.

"Exactly."

"There's only one problem, Reverend," I said, knowing I shouldn't be saying anything. "I told you I believe. That should be enough for you. Judge not, lest ye be judged. Remember?"

"So you believe in the Bible." His eyes narrowed. "All of it?"

"The Bible is the inspired Word of God. Okay?"

"You can't pick and choose, you know."

"Why not?" I glared at him. "You do."

"I believe in the literal Word of God."

"Let's start with your chin." I pointed at it. "It's shaved. Seems to me there's a verse or two in Leviticus that says shaving is an abomination."

"Jesus came to transcend the Law." He drew himself up. "We are no longer bound by it."

"Do you believe in tithing?"

"Of course. God promises to bless us when we do."

"And it's also part of that law you say we are no longer bound by. Funny thing is, when I read the Gospels, Jesus keeps saying give everything, not just ten percent." I pushed forward. "And there's something else people like you never seem to notice. The only time Jesus condemned anybody, it was the religious establishment that he nailed. How often do you preach on Matthew Twenty-Three, huh? You know, about how hypocritical the Pharisees are, putting heavy loads on people's backs and not lifting a finger to help them? And while we're at it, what about the end of Matthew Twenty-Five? When was the last time you gave to the poor?"

"I give to the poor all the time!"

"How about visiting people in prison, or bringing people clothes, or just giving somebody a glass of water? You haven't offered me any. You didn't even offer me a chance to sit down. That's why you're a hypocrite. You're all worrying about the state of my soul, which is none of your damned business, but can't be bothered to offer me a couple basic courtesies." I stopped and put up my hands to ward off his retort. "Now, I'm sorry. I didn't come here to get into a theological debate with you. I'm here because someone was murdered and I don't want to see that happen again to anyone else, including you, by the way." I turned, then turned back. "Oh, and another Scripture you seem to be missing? It's easier for a camel to go through the eye of a needle than for a rich man to get into Heaven. I don't take that literally, by the way. I consider it an excellent use of hyperbole to make a point."

I stalked out of there, trying so hard to calm down. Back in my truck, I got onto the highway and called Esther.

"Is there any chance you can turn that tracker back on?" I asked her.

"Sure. Is this about Van Blinn getting killed?"

"Yep. I don't think we can get away with tracking Reverend Wanzyck's other cars, but since we've got that one already installed, we may as well take advantage of it. Oh, and can you verify whether Wanzyck and his wife really were on a plane from Hawaii yesterday? They arrived here in Los Angeles in the morning. Or so he says."

"Yeah. I should be able to. But Hawaii. That sounds nice."

"He said he was on a retreat." I grunted. "Maybe we should have our next retreat there."

Esther laughed. "Nah. No blackjack tables in Hawaii."

That made me laugh really hard. "Thanks, Esther. I needed that. Wanzyck had to throw that whole cafeteria Christianity thing at me, and I couldn't help it. I threw it right back at him."

"Good for you. It won't do any good, but it's better that he at least hears it."

"Still, I hate losing my temper like that."

"I know. But I would like to have seen it. You're fun when you lose it."

"Be careful," I said with a chuckle. "I'll lose it on you one of these days."

"Well, good luck kicking my ass." Esther laughed.

I laughed hard again. Esther can't kick my ass and she knows it since we spar with each other regularly. As we nattered on, I thanked God for Esther and her friendship. It was what I needed.

Sid was on the phone when I got home that afternoon. I went into the office, where he waved at me, then put the other person on hold.

"I'm talking to Karen Bischorn," he said. "Anything she should know about that ledger that you can think of?"

"No. Not really," I said.

"Why don't you go ahead and clean up, and then we can talk."

"Sounds good."

I went upstairs and got the makeup washed off and my hair unflattened. Then I changed into some nicer jeans and put on a full cotton blouse with all kinds of nine-teenth-century ads on it.

"Well?" I asked Sid when I got back to the office.

He pulled his pocket watch from his pants pocket and opened it. The soft tinkling of Minuet in G made him smile softly.

"Did you have lunch yet?" he asked, leaning back in his desk chair.

"Yeah." I flopped into mine. "I stopped on the way back. You?"

"I got back in plenty of time to eat here, but I didn't have that far to go. So, how was your morning?"

"Trying, at best." I sighed. "I talked to Wanzyck, and then totally went off on him when he started that 'Are you saved?' nonsense."

I repeated the conversation, and Sid chuckled.

"Sounds like he got what he had coming to him."

"Still." I wrinkled my nose. "I'm claiming the higher ground and trying to be Christian, then I go and chew somebody out for not being Christian."

Sid shook his head, smiling. "Lisa, my beloved, you'd find a way to forgive Hitler. What happened at Newport Beach P.D.?"

"Even better." I made a face. "Lieutenant Perrick says that he can't let anyone see anything. That he has orders.

Oh, and Wanzyck said the same thing about the room Van Blinn was in."

"Okay. Something suddenly makes sense." Sid looked at me. "Any hint how Van Blinn was killed?"

"Wanzyck said his wife thought he might have been suffocated. There was no blood, and his tongue was sticking out. How was your morning?"

"I went over to Manotti's office." Sid shrugged. "Went in as David Lawrence." His secondary alias besides Charles Devereaux. "Manotti said that he left town overnight after you called him on Wednesday. We should probably get that confirmed, though."

"Any reason besides good procedure?"

Sid smiled. "I'm fairly sure that he was lying. He seemed unnecessarily nervous the whole time I was talking with him. It could be just that he was talking to a Fed about a murder that he's somewhat connected to."

"Or just a Fed." I thought it over. "You know, he seemed pretty nervous when I talked to him, too. Wanted off the phone really fast, and I went in as a reporter, not a Fed."

"Hm. We may want to lean on him at some point, but I don't think just yet."

"Why not?"

Sid shifted in his chair. "Because I don't know what Lillian wants. It was a nuisance job, for crying out loud. She didn't think it was that important. Now she wants us to find out who killed Van Blinn. That doesn't make sense. And there's something else. As I'm leaving Manotti's office, I pick up a tail, and guess who it is? Good old Noah Taplin."

"Are you sure?"

Sid snorted. "On several levels. I remembered the surveillance photos that Jesse took. Plus, he was doing a lousy job of tailing me. I had him made in less than two minutes." Sid wiped his face with his hand, then cursed. "Is he incompetent. Anyway, so I wait just long enough to get to around the corner from Manotti's office, and I confronted him."

"Euh."

"I can't believe what a whiny weasel he is. He demanded to know why I was tailing him."

"I thought he was tailing you."

Sid rolled his eyes. "Which is what I pointed out to him. He said it was pretty interesting that I was going after Manotti, then made this snide comment that we 53-Q folks were having some serious problems with the guy we were surveilling getting killed right under our noses."

Fifty-Three-Q is Quickline's division name.

"But..." I looked away, trying to figure it out. "Alright. We knew he was onto the surveillance operation, and there's no reason to believe that he didn't know which group was doing it. But how did he peg you as our division? All you did was visit Manotti."

"My best guess?" Sid's brow creased. "He didn't know who I was with and was pretending to know to get confirmation. Which I did not give him. But then he identified himself as Division One, and gave me grief about horning in on his investigation."

"His investigation?" I tried to figure that one out.

"Yep. So I offered to share information. And he gets all huffy and says that he's on top of it and doesn't need any help. In fact, he's fixed it so that we'll have to ask him for help if we want anything."

I groaned. "Like information from the NBPD. Perrick said he was under orders."

Sid cursed again.

"Sid, I just thought of something." I pressed my lips together as I tried to find the words for what was going through my brain. "I don't know if I told you, but the sliding glass door was off its track. I saw it."

Sid nodded. "And that's usually a significant weak spot, unless someone put a bar or something in the track to keep it closed."

"But the cops and the security company didn't see it when the alarm was triggered that night."

"Huh?"

"Wanzyck said that his mother-in-law told them everything was okay."

"That's odd." Sid folded his arms as he thought it over. "Why didn't they do a more thorough check?"

"I don't know." I felt my face scrunch up. "But it might explain why the NBPD is so eager to go along with those orders they got. Who would want it to get out that they screwed up the death of the congressman so badly?"

"You know. That makes sense." Sid blinked and rubbed around his eye sockets. He wears contact lenses because he's so near-sighted, and has to be careful how he rubs his eyes lest he knock a lens off-kilter. "Okay. Now what do we do?"

"Maybe we should try to look at other suspects," I said. "What about decoding that ledger? I mean, it's possible that Van Blinn's death was connected to him trying to find who killed Sheila, isn't it?"

"There is that. That's why I called Karen Bischorn just now." Sid's brow creased in thought. "I can't imagine why he'd have done so, but is it possible that Jay Fedders doesn't want anyone to know who killed Sheila?"

"He's too young to have killed Sheila," I said. "He's not that old."

"True." Sid got up and began pacing. "But what about this idea? I'll concede it's pretty far-fetched, but what if Fedders is hoping to make some money on the story, and he'll make significantly more if the mystery remains unsolved?"

"Or maybe Van Blinn was the culprit and Fedders got all angry and offed him out of a sense of justice?"

Sid's eyebrow quirked up. "Honestly?"

"It isn't any crazier than figuring Fedders could make some worthwhile money on leaving the case unsolved."

Sid sighed. "Okay. Points conceded to your side. Now what?"

"That, my beloved, remains a very good question."

January 21 – 23, 1989

(Sid's Voice)

I took Darby with me to tune Nacho Pulido's piano that Saturday. We stopped at the music school first, where Mr. Pulido and his brother were pushing the small brown upright up a ramp onto the back of a beat-up pickup truck. What Stella hadn't told the Pulidos was that she had bought the piano second-hand from someone else, refurbished it, and was probably going to "forget" that the Pulidos had it.

Not all of Stella's students were underprivileged kids, but many of them were. Getting music lessons at all was a big deal for them. At the same time, you don't want to tell people who are working their asses off to feed their families that they're not doing enough for their kids. So Stella scoured the newspapers for used pianos and other instruments, got them fixed up, then "loaned" them to the students who needed them. She could have bought the instruments new, but used ones supported the fiction that people just dumped them on her.

Darby and I had a good time helping get the piano set up in the tiny apartment, then tuning it.

"You're getting really good at tuning," I told him as we rode back to Pasadena and his house.

"It's fun," said Darby, with a shrug. "Hey, Uncle Sid, why didn't you become a professional tuner? Mr. Galvez, the city orchestra conductor? He told me that you can make some pretty good money tuning pianos."

"You can," I said. "And I picked up a fair amount of cash that way. But it takes time to build your clientele, and I needed my restaurant job to make rent, plus going to school. I might have kept at it, but by the time I had enough clients to ditch waiting tables, I'd inherited my money from Stella's father, and there was no point. Besides, it can be pretty boring work."

"I suppose if that's all you're doing."

And we fell silent.

The next day was Super Bowl Sunday, and the whole Fam-Damily gathered at Mae and Neil's place, including Lisa and Mae's parents. Daddy and Nick had a particularly good time since the Forty-Niners were in the big game. Nick isn't much of a football fan - he lives and breathes baseball. But he was born and lived in the Bay Area before I got custody of him when he was twelve, so those are the teams he roots for. Daddy and Mama live in the Lake Tahoe area, so Daddy generally roots for Bay Area teams.

Even with the annoyances of the week before, I was in a pretty good mood by Monday morning.

I picked Stella up fairly early for our trip to San Diego and our meeting with Dr. Rhoda Farber. Stella is not the most talkative person in the world, but she was unusually quiet that morning.

"What are you thinking about?" I finally asked as we drove past San Juan Capistrano.

She gazed at the ocean to the right of us. "You know, Nick loves the ocean."

"He most certainly does."

"So did my sister." She fell silent again, watching the waves. Then she looked at me. "Sid, do you ever wonder how much genetics plays into who we are or become?"

"Hm." I thought about it. "I didn't use to. But I guess I've been wondering a little bit about it over the past few years. Why do you ask?"

"You're very much like her." Stella looked back out the window again.

"That's what Tina Goetz said."

"I don't mean that in a bad way. Or about the sex."

"Goetz did." I chuckled. "About the sex, I mean."

"I know what I said back when you were a teen." Stella sighed. "But that's not how you're like my... Your mother. You screwed around because you liked it. I don't think Sheila liked sex. She certainly didn't like men, although I don't think she was a lesbian."

"That was probably being molested and her work."

"Probably." She looked at me again, her eyes piercing. "But Sheila was very logical. She could analyze a situation from all the different angles and come up with some amazing solutions. I remember when she was pregnant and I was still teaching, there was a dust-up at the school where I worked. Sheila figured out what the issue was and even came up with a way for me to deal with it. You'd do the same thing with your buddies at school. Loser would come up with some crazy scheme, and you'd not only figure out how to pull it off, but also how to get away with it."

I laughed. "How did you know I was doing that?"

"You think I couldn't listen?" Stella smiled. "Besides, Loser would tell me what you and Tom and the others were up to."

"That scum bucket."

"Oh, he was so proud of you boys, that you were putting one over on The Man." Stella smiled, then blinked her eyes. "I felt awful when I heard he'd been killed."

I nodded. "Me, too."

Loser had gotten drafted right around the same time as I had. We'd both been sent to Vietnam, and part of my trauma was that I'd survived, and so many others, like Loser, hadn't.

"Anyway," Stella cleared her throat. Me going in when I was drafted had been a serious sore point between us. "Loser once told me that you'd be a great chess champion because you could see all the pieces on the board and which way they could all go."

"Oh." I swallowed.

Stella's eyebrow lifted. "What's the matter with that?"

"Nothing." I riveted my eyes directly ahead. "Someone last summer said the same thing about me."

"Well, it's true. And it was true about Sheila."

"Hmm."

We lapsed into silence again, and when we did speak, it was only about trivial topics.

Dr. Rhoda Farber's office was in a complex of medical offices. Her room was comfortably laid out and featured a soft leather sofa, and large wooden desk with a leather desk chair.

I know Lisa gets a little annoyed with me when I refer to a woman as a great broad. {Not always. - ljw} But that is exactly what Farber was. In her early sixties, she'd gained some weight around her middle, and her short red hair was laced with gray. She was dressed in a pant suit and was utterly comfortable in her own skin. Any bullshit you gave her, you'd get right back, and in your face, too.

"It's good to meet both of you," she said, as Stella and I settled on the couch. Farber wheeled her desk chair to face us, spread her knees, and leaned forward. "As I understand it, this is about my infamous past."

"It's like I told you on the phone last week," Stella said. "We found Jane Smith's ledger, and we're hoping to find out who killed my sister with it."

"Unfortunately," I cut in before Stella could get herself in any more trouble. "The names of Jane's clients were written in code. So we're hoping you remember some of the names so that we can track them down."

Farber frowned. "Oh. Let's see... Most of them would be dead by now, I would think. There were a few young guys. Jimmy Van Blinn, of course. He was carrying the torch for Sheila. Warren Halstead. Um. Allan Malfy. Mason Brightman. Paul West. Wait. Brightman. He could get pretty rough with us. When Sheila was killed, I immediately thought Brightman had done it. But there's no way of knowing that I can tell."

"Do you remember what happened that day?" I asked.

"Oh, yeah." Farber grimaced. "It was terrible. Tina found her. I was in my room, getting ready for that night's date, and heard all the screaming. So I went into Sheila's room, and there she was. It was a mess. Worse yet, Jane got real scared. When she told us two weeks later that she'd sold the house and was moving to California, I thought I'd follow her. Only when I did, I found out that she'd gotten out of the life."

"Is that when you got out?" Stella asked.

"Uh, no." Farber smiled. "It took me another five or six years to do that. One of my johns talked me into going to college. And I discovered psychology, and am now helping other women get out. In addition to working with the normal neuroses."

"Can you tell me about Sheila?" I asked.

"She was the usual, poor thing. Totally cut off from her emotions. It didn't register then, but later I figured she was probably sexually abused as a kid. Most of us were, by the way. Not all of us, but most." Farber looked at Stella. "You're the older sister, right?"

"That's me."

Farber nodded. "She complained a lot about being under your thumb. So I asked her one time why she didn't leave. She just said she wouldn't. But again, with that good old twenty-twenty hindsight, I think she was afraid of being alone."

"Hmm." Stella's brow creased. "I do believe you're right. Sheila always had to be the center of attention."

"Probably the only way she felt validated." Farber smiled and shrugged. "But don't feel bad. Sheila was hardly the only messed-up girl in that house. There were several who had nothing nice to say about anybody. One who I now think may even have been an actual psychopath. She was even more cut off from her emotions than Sheila was. And another I'm pretty sure had a full-blown psychosis. She seriously believed that we were all having fun and that we were in a great life. Talk about a break with reality." She stopped. "By the way, none of what I just said should be construed as an official diagnosis or medical opinion. I'm just guessing. You know?"

"Well, of course," said Stella. "I'm just thankful that you were willing to talk to us."

We said goodbye shortly after that and got back on the freeway to Los Angeles.

(Lisa's Voice)

The one good thing that Monday morning was that I was able to make some headway on my reading. Then, just after lunch, Kathy came by with a folder of papers.

"The congressman's financials are clean," she announced, holding Keshon. "Honestly, Lisa. My personal books don't look this good."

"Is that suspicious?"

"So-so." She laughed and shrugged. "I'm mostly just jealous." She put the folder on my desk, then slid onto the office couch. "But Jacob Van Blinn's financials are not nearly as pristine."

"Who's Jacob Van Blinn? A relative?"

"The congressman's older brother. He's a banker in New York," Kathy said. "But it's a straight-up bank rather than an S&L. And there's nothing serious on the personal side. Just some deposits that don't make sense."

"Why did you look at the congressman's older brother?"

"Why not?" Kathy made a face, then set Keshon on the floor to toddle about. She shrugged and smiled. "Okay. Maybe James was a little too clean. It's not very common, but sometimes people will use relatives' accounts to hide money. But that's usually something that happens at the last minute, like when the auditor is on your doorstep. And it doesn't always work because of people like me, who double-check the relatives' accounts. The thing is, there should have been some coordinating withdrawals in the congressman's account, and there aren't."

"Which means that Jacob may be misbehaving, but James probably wasn't."

"That's what it looks like." Kathy shrugged. "On the other hand, James got killed. So I have to wonder if there was something else going on."

I bit my lip. "There was. Sort of. It was a political witch hunt. Somebody at a high level wanted to use our intelligence assets to go after Van Blinn. Our supervisors were furious."

"It's a good thing you didn't tell Jesse this." Kathy shuddered. "He'd've been on the ceiling."

"So were we." I sighed.

"Why are you telling me now?" Kathy asked.

"Because now you have Need to Know." I caught Keshon as he tried opening my desk drawers and put him on my lap. "We need to look into what was behind Van Blinn getting killed."

Kathy's face got that worried look. "You don't think the people who wanted us surveilling Van Blinn set him up to get killed, do you?"

"It doesn't make sense that they would. What would they gain by it? Besides, killing people gets messy, especially public types like Van Blinn. Not only are we supposed to be looking into it, there's a second agency involved, and that's in addition to regular law enforcement. That makes it awfully hard to keep secret."

"True." Kathy got up and got Keshon from my arms. "Well, I'm going to keep following the money, but my impression is that we're not going to find much."

"I have to agree." I sighed. "But it's better to be thorough."

Kathy left, and then I got paged. It was Lillian. So I paged Sid that I'd get it, and called her back.

"It's about those orders the Newport Beach police got," Lillian told me after we'd done the code verification ritual. "Taplin definitely arranged them."

"I'm not surprised." I drummed my fingers on the desk. "Did we tell you that I talked to the two of Van Blinn's donors out here? One, Earl Manotti, told me that Taplin hadn't spoken to him. Then, after Van Blinn was killed, Sid went in under his Lawrence alias, and Manotti said that he was out of town the night that Van Blinn was killed. Then Taplin found Sid and said that we'd need help from him if we were going after Van Blinn's killer."

"What about the other fellow? A Bright something or other?"

"Mason Brightman." I gagged a little. "What a jerk. I talked to him before Van Blinn's death, and I'll definitely be checking his alibi for that night. But get this, he not only knew Taplin, Brightman said Taplin was how he got the goods on Van Blinn about Sheila Hackbirn dying. Never mind that Brightman was one of the customers at the whorehouse, and probably suspected Van Blinn, just like everyone else did."

"As in, Brightman didn't need the goods on Van Blinn because he already had them." Lillian groaned. "But didn't you tell me that Taplin was warning Van Blinn about the surveillance?"

"Yeah. Either Brightman was lying or Taplin was playing everybody off of each other."

Lillian snorted. "I would think the latter except that Taplin isn't bright enough for that kind of game. Admittedly, the one thing the man does well is make friends, but to play them off each other? That takes some understanding of nuance that would completely escape Taplin."

"Um, is it possible that the people who set Van Blinn up for the surveillance were also behind killing him?"

"I doubt it." Lillian sighed. "I'm not saying someone hasn't tried it before. But there's enough rivalry going on between the agencies, and enough investigative talent, that it's very difficult to get away with it."

"Because the first place you look is the victim's enemies."

"Correct." She sighed again. "And speaking of rivalries, Taplin is up to his ears in this one. Not only had he heard about the surveillance, he was trying to make Quickline look bad because we were doing the job when Van Blinn died."

"Oh, no! We called the surveillance because we had the evidence that Van Blinn wasn't doing anything."

"And what are the odds you could have caught the killer in the act? We told you to take a light hand, and you followed orders."

"Still." I made a face. "How much trouble are you in?"

Lillian chuckled. "It's sticky. But I've been in much worse and lived to tell about it. So don't worry about me. Or Henry, for that matter. We're where we're at because we know how to play this game. Taplin doesn't."

"But he makes friends."

"Nuance, dear. He has no clue how to keep them." Lillian chuckled again. "Let's just say that I'm not the only person who wants Taplin's ass in a sling. I'm just the one who wants it the most at the moment."

I wasn't feeling entirely reassured when I hung up a few minutes later, but I didn't get much time to think about it. Esther called, so I invited her over for my second and her first lunch, then did a little more reading until she got there.

Conchetta, our housekeeper, had made her delicious vegetarian chili with homemade tortillas. I got the dishes into the office so that Esther and I could talk freely. Conchetta has some sort of clearance, but we don't let her hear much, either.

"You look smug," I told Esther as we sprinkled more hot pepper flakes on the chili that was already darned spicy.

"We got one on NBPD." She grinned, then sniffled. "I've got an approximate time of death and cause of death, plus who NBPD is probably looking at."

"How did you get all that?" I gaped, then swallowed. "Esther, did you bug the Newport Beach police?"

"No!" Esther made a face. "That's way too much work. I found out who was in charge of the security contract for the complex and made a sales call for one of my cameras."

Esther's visible business is making high tech home and business security equipment. It's incredibly useful for us.

"And he talked to you about it."

"Well, you know," Esther said around a mouthful of tortilla. "I had to ask about what challenges he had. So we started bitching about clients, and he told me about how they had a murder at one of their properties, and he's working his ass off because his guy followed protocol when the old lady inside told him and the cops that nothing was wrong and there had to have been a false alarm."

"They didn't think the alarm was enough reason to go in?"

Esther shook her head. "It's not. They can't go in unless there's a clear danger. You know, someone calling for help. Even the cops have a hard time justifying going in without that. And the old lady there, she's not acting hinky or scared. In fact, she was flirting with the guard."

"And you're sure this is the Van Blinn murder?"

"Had to be. Okay. I asked, too." She snickered. "He didn't say it was, but had to show off how much he knew about it. That's how I got the time the alarm went off, which should be close to the time of death. He also followed up with the P.D. the next day and got the probable cause of death and some of the suspects."

"So what do they think happened?" I put my hand in front of my mouth to cover a burp. "Excuse me."

Esther flat-out burped. "Someone got the sliding glass door off the track. It's not hard to do, you know, and the cops found the scratch marks on the track. The alarm got triggered at 11:28 p.m. That gave the perp about ten minutes to suffocate Van Blinn, then get out, which is tight, but doable. The guard first went around to the back of the house, but all he saw was the screen door standing open and the sliding glass door a little out of alignment. That's not unusual. And what he was really looking for were signs of somebody inside, which he didn't see."

"That's interesting."

"So he goes around front to the door, knocks and all that, and the old lady opens the door and says there's nobody there. And that's when the cops showed, and she says the same thing, only by then she's getting cranky because it's the middle of the night and she's tired. So they all left, filed the report, and the next morning, Mrs. Wanzyck finds the stiff, and it all goes to hell."

"Hm." I thought it over as I munched on some beans. "What about the suspects?"

"Not anybody specific." Esther rolled her eyes. "They're going with the burglar being surprised that Van Blinn was there, but that doesn't make sense. He wasn't hit over the head or shot. Just suffocated. And it happened quickly. I suppose it's possible that the killer was still in the room when the security people came by. But how could he have known the cops wouldn't come into the room?"

"Maybe he was hoping they wouldn't," I said. "Or just decided to brazen it out. It's not like we haven't done that before."

Esther made a face, but didn't say anything. We finished eating, then she took off and I went back to reading. Sid got home soon after.

"How did it go?" I asked as we sat in the breakfast room eating chili. Okay. It was my third bowl.

He told me about the conversation, but didn't think there were any conclusions to be drawn. I had to agree.

"How are you feeling about all of it?" I asked.

Sid thought about it for a second. "Mostly good. You know, it was kind of nice to spend some one-on-one time with Stella. And the funny thing is, I learned more about my mother from her than anything Dr. Farber said."

"Sounds like you did well." I smiled at him.

We finished eating and went back to the office, where I turned to my reading and class prep, and Sid did some freelance work. Until he got a call. He talked for a couple minutes, then put the caller on hold.

"I've just gotten invited to Van Blinn's funeral," he told me, then sighed. "It's Wednesday. Jacob Van Blinn really wants me to go."

"What if Taplin's there? He'll find out your real name, and I can't see that being a good thing."

"You're right." Sid cursed. "Unless he already knows it. You know who might know if he does or not?"

"Lillian or Henry?"

"Or both."

Henry didn't answer his phone - he frequently doesn't. So Sid called Lillian, who was thrilled about Sid's invitation to the funeral.

"We are concerned about Taplin finding out my real name, however," Sid said. "It will be very hard to use an alias there."

"You've got a point." Then Lillian let out a positively evil chuckle. "I think I know exactly how to handle this. Sid, why don't you go ahead and make arrangements to go to the funeral? I will page you if, for some reason, we can't get Taplin out of the way."

"Are you sure?"

"Oh, yes. As I told Lisa earlier today, I'm not the only person who wants Taplin's ass in a sling. Not by a long shot."

January 25 – 26, 1989

(Sid's Voice)

The worst part of going to New York for the Van Blinn funeral was that Lisa didn't go with me. She offered, but I convinced her that it would be better not to cancel her classes. She grumbled that she should never have started her PhD, and I had to remind her that it had been one of her big dreams. As it turned out a few years later, it was a damned good thing she'd stayed focused on her degree.

The problem is that Lisa loved being a spy even more than she loved teaching English composition. So when those two occupations came into conflict with each other, she could get a little cranky.

I flew out on Tuesday, after our morning run and getting the boys to school. What with the time change and all, it was either that or take a red-eye flight overnight, and Lisa convinced me that being tired would not help the investigation. Stella had been thrilled about my going to the funeral, and not only offered to cover my piano students, she tried to give me a list of people to look for. A list, I reminded her, that I already had.

The flight was uneventful, and I got downtown and settled in my hotel in time to go to dinner with Steve Parsons and Ray Spinoza, the floater team for the Green Line. We met at a lovely place down in Greenwich Village.

Ray had dark hair, liberally sprinkled with gray, and wore wire-rimmed glasses. Steve was taller, but with a bit of a gut, and receding blond hair. We chatted about life in general until our food came.

"I gotta tell you," Steve said as he cut up some chicken parmigiana. "We were shocked to hear that Fedders guy telling Van Blinn about you."

"I can imagine," I said. "How did that happen?"

"Van Blinn got all excited," Steve said. "I could have sworn he was going to wet his pants. He hangs up, then calls his friend Earline, gets the invite to stay at her son-in-law's, then has his secretary call the airlines. Next thing you know, he's out on the West Coast."

"Which is when we were asked to take over." Sid made a face.

"And your mother was a hooker?" Steve asked, grinning.

"Easy, honey," Ray said with amused irritation.

Steve was a terrific guy, but not the soul of tact. He used to drive Lillian nuts.

"It doesn't bother me," I said, laughing. "You know I'm shameless."

"And I thought I had mommy problems," Steve said with an exaggerated roll of the eyes. "Could not believe that her baby boy is gay. I'm, like, 'Ma, I sing soprano, for God's sakes. You couldn't figure it out?' She just completely freaked. And the rest of the family."

"Sounds rough," I said.

"Well, yeah," Steve said. "But it's not my fault they're all assholes. My sister-in-law won't even let us into their house. She's convinced we have AIDS and we'll give it to the kids. Thank God for Ray's mom. She's an angel.

Ray smiled. "My mom is great. No siblings, but it was always just the two of us until Steve came along."

"No father?" I asked.

"Nah." Ray shrugged. "He died when I was an infant."

"That's too bad," I replied.

"It's how it was. I didn't really think too much about it. I knew other kids had fathers." Ray suddenly sniggered. "The worst of it was all their dads wanted to make it up to me that I didn't have a father. Like it was some sort of deadly disease."

I laughed loudly. "God, I hate that! I have never been able to figure out why every man I meet wants to be my surrogate dad."

"You don't have a father?" Steve asked, his head cocked to one side.

"Nope. It literally says unknown on my birth certificate." I paused. "In fact, now that I think about it, I'm technically an orphan."

"Poor fellow," Steve sang, and I busted up again.

It's a line from The Pirates of Penzance, and it turned out that Steve and Ray had seen the Broadway version with Kevin Kline several years before, and several times more since. I'd not only seen the film, Lisa had the video tape and got it out every so often.

Some time after, I gave them the names that I'd gotten from Dr. Farber, and they agreed to find what they could. I went back to the hotel and also did some looking through the local phone directory, but didn't come up with anything. Then I called Lisa and Nick.

The call and the time spent with the guys did me no end of good. There was just something about the shared experience of being raised by a woman with no father that helped me get a new perspective on the way things were going. Which was a very good thing, because the funeral was not fun, and I have been to a few fun ones.

It wasn't particularly dismal. I'd certainly been to worse. It was a full Episcopalian service, which reminded me a lot of the Catholic mass, which made me miss Lisa all the more. She's Catholic. In fact, she met Frank Lonnergan and the rest of our team at church. I first made friends with Frank. And the next thing I knew, all six of us became close, and I was playing the organ for the choir. As an atheist. And being at Van Blinn's funeral, I couldn't help but think of the incredible turn my life had taken when I'd rescued Lisa from a blind date, then hired her as my secretary (visibly) and associate in the spy biz.

The crowd in the church was huge. Politicians of all stripes, movers and shakers from the world of business, even a few actors. News cameras had been set up outside the front of the church, and I was glad I was able to find a side entrance. At the end of the service, a receiving line was set up in the vestibule. I went through because I figured, given that Jacob had personally invited me, it was the least I could do, and that was my intent.

It had been announced that the graveside service was for family members only. I was relieved. I'd have an excuse to get out of there and get the earliest flight back to L.A. I could. Only when I introduced myself to Jacob Van Blinn, he asked that I go to the graveside service.

"I'm not a member of the family," I said.

"I know." His gray eyes were as watery as his brother's had been, but he was considerably stockier with hair that was suspiciously dark brown. I looked closer, and, yeah, it was a toupee, but a damn good one. "I'll explain later."

I agreed to go.

At the gravesite, there was the usual. I held to the back of the group and waited until the bronzed casket had been lowered into the ground. Jacob turned a minute later and caught my eye, then nodded toward a nearby tombstone. I made my way there and waited while he spoke with his wife, a small woman wearing black.

"I'm glad you could make it here," Jacob said to me as he walked up.

"I'm glad I could be here," I said, watching him carefully.

He seemed weighed down. "There is a problem that I hope you can help us with."

"I don't understand."

"We need someone close. Who has a stake in our family." He held up his hand against my protest. "I know we are total strangers. But my brother was very impressed by you, and while he understood that you did not feel the same way, he also felt a sincere connection to you." Jacob blinked and shook his head, then looked back at his wife. "Jimmy was so happy when I last talked to him. He'd called the morning before..." Jacob blinked again. "He was going to amend his will to include you. Just a small bequest and I don't know the whole of it. He said he wanted Sheila's son to have that much. That he owed it to her memory." Jacob looked at me. "I must confess that while I knew Sheila, and she was certainly quite a pleasant young woman, her, eh, profession notwithstanding, I never understood Jimmy's complete devotion to her."

"Didn't you discourage your brother?"

"Oh, yes." He blinked at me, then smiled wanly. "I know she was your mother, but she was hardly suitable. It wasn't surprising. Jimmy could be very rebellious, especially when he was younger. And he had quite a temper. In fact, my father made a point of contacting the police department because he was afraid that Jimmy had killed Sheila."

"I heard that somebody stopped the investigation." I said, the ire creeping into my voice.

"He was trying to protect our family." Jacob shrugged. "But I can no longer excuse what Father did. Jimmy never forgave him for it. And as the years passed and Jimmy's devotion did not ease up, I had to believe that he did not kill Sheila." Jacob looked back at his wife. "It was an amazing thing, really. Jimmy said that he could not marry. That he could not imagine loving or even being with another woman. Can you imagine being that deeply in love?"

"Actually, I can." I smiled. "I am that deeply in love with my wife."

"Oh." His eyes blinked rapidly, and I could almost see him trying to figure that one out. "Well. Then you will understand why I need your help. After all, this could touch your family, as well. Jimmy had a notebook. Well, quite a few of them, actually. He wrote in them constantly. Hid a lot of them. We have gone through both of his apartments and believe we have found almost all. But the one he was writing in at the time of his death. That we can't get. We asked the police department involved, and they said that they had turned over all of his personal effects and that there was no notebook."

"And you're worried that there's something damaging in the one that the cops didn't find."

"It's always possible." Jacob colored up a little. "We read some of them, and there were a few embarrassing observations."

I had to act casual, but it was not easy tamping down the excitement I felt.

"I'm not a cop," I said, feigning helplessness. "What can I do?"

"You at least live near there. Maybe you can get the police to cooperate and let you in the room."

"Why not ask Earline or her son-in-law?"

Jacob cleared his throat. "I did ask Mrs. Wilson. Well, not in any specific sense. I have to be honest. I suspect Mrs. Wilson would use the notebook to her own profit. And her son-in-law might not intend any harm, but he would see to his own family's benefit rather than ours."

"Okay." I felt the buzzing of my pager, so I pulled my watch from my pants and opened it. "Well, I'm afraid I have to catch a plane. I'll do what I can."

We exchanged business cards, and I found my way to the front of the cemetery and hailed a passing cab. I waited until we were on our way back to Manhattan to check my pager. It was Lisa and she needed me to call her back Priority Two. When I got to the hotel where I'd stayed the night before, I called her. I'd stashed my overnight bag with the hotel concierge after I'd checked out, and as I waited for the concierge to get the bag, Lisa got on the line.

Jay Fedders had called. He'd seen me at the funeral and was hoping that I'd call Lisa before I left New York.

"Okay. I'll call him," I said, with a decided lack of enthusiasm. "Unless Fedders has something really good, I'll be flying back this evening."

"Good. I can't wait."

"Neither can I," I said, thinking about the only woman I could imagine loving, living with, making love to. Yes, I was (and am) that deeply in love with my sweet Lisa.

I called from the hotel lobby. Fedders was in his office.

"Sorry I didn't catch you at the funeral," I told him. "It was quite a crowd."

"It sure was." Fedders laughed. "You're right on top of Newport Beach. What happened?"

"I only know what the news says, and there wasn't a lot of coverage. The cops are, apparently, keeping a really tight lid on it."

"Huh." Fedders yawned. "So does that mean they have no clue who killed Van Blinn and are trying to cover that up, or that they know damned well who did, but need to make sure their asses are covered before announcing it?"

I couldn't help chuckling. "Your guess is as good as mine."

I briefly toyed with the idea of sending Fedders after Taplin, but realized that it would not be a good idea.

Fedders yawned again. "Sorry about that. Just got in this morning. I've been out in San Francisco since Wednesday for the big consumer electronics show." He yawned again. "I mean, following up on it. It's a seriously big deal for us, you know."

I thought about it. "Yeah. I guess it is. I don't really do much on video games, though."

"I know. Anyway, I had to come back for the big funeral." Fedders laughed loudly. "This is turning into one hell of a story, isn't it? Nothing like being on the ground floor."

"It's pretty cool," I said. "But I have to get going. Don't want to miss my flight home."

"Sure thing. Talk to you later."

We hung up and I had the hotel concierge book me on the earliest flight to L.A., then just barely made it to Kennedy airport on time.

(Lisa's Voice)

That Tuesday and Wednesday were not good days for me. Sid had insisted that there wasn't that much to be gotten from the trip, so there wasn't any point in my being there. And he was right. He was also right that my PhD work was very important, too, and that I shouldn't neglect it if I didn't have to. But I would rather have been chasing down potential suspects. That's all there is to it.

Then there's the reality of Nick. The poor kid worries about us. Not all the time. But he always knows when what we're doing is something for the side business, and he knows that it can get dangerous. He doesn't freak completely, but he's not happy, and certainly wasn't that Tuesday and Wednesday.

And I wasn't happy, either, especially by Wednesday morning. The truth is, neither Sid nor I sleeps well if we haven't had sex. So, between being groggy, having stacks of papers to grade, and even more reading and a progress report to write for my Shakespeare project, plus trying to keep Nick from getting too upset, it was not my best day.

When Sid called from New York that he would be on his way soon, I was thrilled. Nick even more so. Darby got home from violin lessons shortly after. Both he and Nick had gotten their homework done at school and were talking about a trip to Magic Mountain, possibly to celebrate Nick's birthday in mid-February.

"Then you'll have to find a way to pay for it," I told them at dinner.

"Aw, Aunt Lisa, come on," groaned Darby. "Maybe it could be Nick's birthday present."

"If we do it as a family outing, maybe," I said, grinning. "Or you could find a way to pay for it yourself."

Nick and Darby both looked at each other and rolled their eyes. But after dinner, they landed in the library and started comparing notes on expenses and their respective incomes for the next few weeks and months.

Given that Sid and I are fairly wealthy, you'd think we'd be more willing to indulge Nick, Darby, and his siblings. And there are times when we do. But Sid wants Nick to be able to stay wealthy, and Mae and Neil don't want their kids picking up Neil's lousy money sense. Neil's dad has bailed the two of them out numerous times over the years, and it really embarrasses and infuriates Mae.

So when the boys were fourteen, Mae, Neil, Sid, and I got together and agreed on some ground rules, then the four of us had a long talk with each of the three sets of grandparents (both actual and functional). Stella and my dad were completely on board, as was Neil's mother. The rest went along with it because we were being very sensible and fair.

To Breanna, 8/24/00

Topic of the Day: Managing Money

Why were you so surprised that I'm worth so much? Come on. Darby and me financed that entire trip to New Zealand. I bought a house on the Venice canals last summer, all cash. You don't do those sorts of things without serious money in the bank. And I don't blow through money indiscriminately. That's thanks to my Dad, who let me do just that. I only did it once, believe me.

The summer I was fifteen, Grandpa Wycherly hired me to work at his resort as a busboy. Oh man, I hated that job! But by the time I was able to quit, my bank account was really full. Well, it was more money of my own than I'd had at one time.

Then Dad told me I could do whatever I wanted with the money - I'd earned it, so I had the right to. Only it had to last through Christmas, and that I wouldn't be getting my allowance until then. Yeah, I was pissed. But Dad pointed out that I didn't have to pay rent, or buy food, or pay for school. Couldn't argue with that.

He also gave me my own credit card, only there was one little catch. It was for emergencies only. Like if I got hurt and had to pay for the emergency room when they weren't home. Or I was stranded somewhere and needed a cab. Serious stuff. He said I could use it for other stuff, but if it wasn't an emergency, I would have to pay him back.

Still, I had this full bank account and decided I deserved a splurge. So I took Josh and Darby to Disneyland. We had a blast. We had lunch at the Blue Bayou. We ate a boatload of popcorn and ice cream bars, bought hats and t-shirts. We basically went apeshit. Only I hadn't brought enough cash, and right before lunch, I ran out. What the hell. I had a credit card. I'd just pay Dad back.

When Dad got the bill, he pointed out all the charges I'd made. I nearly had a heart attack. Half my bank account gone in one afternoon. Dad was cool and told me he'd done the same thing when he'd first inherited his money. But he did not bail me out and had set it up with the grandparents that they wouldn't either.

I paid him back and struggled along that semester. Finally, in November, Stella hired me to sweep up at her music school. Darby was already working there for the same reason. He kept blowing through his allowance, and his parents weren't giving him any more. Stella also taught the two of us how to make a budget and invest our money. So, while I started with a good pile, thanks to a trust fund Dad had set up for me, both he and Stella made sure I knew how to make it work for me. And that's why I have money.

By the time the boys had come up with a plan for the amusement park that did not involve going with the Whole Fam-Damily, it was getting close to nine. I was glad of the distraction for Nick's sake.

Nick and I both heard the garage door opening and ran to the back of the house. Darby sauntered along behind us, arriving as Sid came in through the door from the utility room to the garage. The boys both got hugs, then sent to bed.

Sid paused just long enough to place on my lips a soft, innocent kiss that was at the same time filled with passion. Never mind how much we wanted to be loving each other, we took our time going up the stairs and into our bedroom. Why not? Taking our time was half the fun.

Later, we snuggled together. Sid, having slept on the plane, was not that sleepy. Me? I was drowsy, but still coherent.

"Did Nick and Darby get their homework done?" Sid asked.

"They got it done at school." I chuckled. "They spent the evening trying to figure out how to finance a day at Magic Mountain and still have money at the end of the semester."

Sid laughed softly. "So the lesson stuck. I'm glad."

"Hard to imagine not after last fall," I said.

"It wasn't guaranteed." Sid grew thoughtful. "That's one thing I always appreciated about Stella. She let me learn the hard way. She wasn't going to let me do hard drugs or seriously hurt myself. But when I was ten, she let me get drunk after warning me that it would make me really sick. After that, I had to believe what she said about heroin and LSD. And when I got that girl pregnant when I was a sophomore in high school, Stella got her taken care of by a good doctor. But I had to pay Stella back for the abortion. It was my responsibility, and I was an idiot if I didn't keep myself covered from then on. And I did." Sid held me even closer. "Then, when Nick arrived, you were very loving, but didn't let him get away with anything. And I'd certainly seen Mae and Neil doing the same with their kids. It hit me. Stella was a pretty good parent. She wasn't perfect. It would have been nice to feel how much she really wanted me. Or to know all she kept back from me. I do not want to repeat her mistakes. At the same time, what she got right, I want to do for Nick."

"You're not going to let him get drunk, are you?"

Sid laughed and winced. "Okay, that may not have been one of Stella's better moves. But I can understand it. There was so much of that crap floating around where I was growing up. She had to do something that would make an impression to keep me safe from it. It's sort of like us training Nick in the business. A lot of people would think we shouldn't do something like that, but given our circumstances, it's the best way to keep him safe."

I was feeling a little more awake, so I asked him about his day. We both wondered how we were going to find that notebook, but then he fell asleep, and I rolled over and fell asleep, too.

The next day was filled with school and teaching. Then that night, as we watched the early news, we found out that Tina Goetz had been murdered in her living room.

January 27 – 30, 1986

We got the call around eight the next morning. Jay Fedders wanted Sid to go to a press conference put on by the San Marino Police Department. Sid grinned and asked me to join him.

"We need to work this one together," he said.

"I'll say. It's been too long." I made a face. "Think we'll be okay if I go as myself rather than Agent Devereaux?"

"Should be," he said. "You know, it's probably better if you are yourself. What if Leslie's there?"

"You're right." I sighed a little.

My best friend from high school is local TV reporter Leslie Bowman, which can make things interesting at times. As it happened, Leslie wasn't there. The station she works for sent someone else, which was fine with us.

San Marino is a quiet suburb just south of Pasadena, and one of the wealthiest areas in Southern California. The conference was held outside on the street next to the front of the City Hall, a large two-story edifice, probably built sometime in the '20s or '30s. Police Chief Dwayne Constanza stepped up to the small podium right on time. He didn't look too happy. No surprise. A citizen murdered in her own home made the neighbors antsy, and these were wealthy neighbors, probably used to getting their own way.

"Thank you for coming," the chief droned. "At approximately two p.m. yesterday afternoon, officers responded to a call from the housekeeper, who had found the house's owner, Mrs. Tina Goetz, deceased in her living room, apparently the victim of a violent attack. There are no suspects at this time, however, there has been a suggestion that Mrs. Goetz's death might be connected to the recent murder of Congressman Van Blinn, as she was a former associate of the congressman many years ago."

Sid and I glanced at each other, wondering if Fedders had made the suggestion.

"Officers have canvassed the neighborhood, but there are no witnesses thus far," Chief Constanza continued. "We are asking the public for any information they might have relating to this crime. Any questions?"

"How strong is the link to the Van Blinn murder?" someone in the small crowd of reporters asked.

"Fairly weak," the chief replied.

"Is there a cause of death?"

"Nothing official."

And so it went on, the reporters asking for more details, the chief declining to answer. Finally, he offered assurances that his department was working full time and that patrols in the area would be stepped up. As the other reporters packed up their cameras and/or their notebooks, Sid nodded at me and we headed around back to the police station itself. Sid slid on a pair of glasses that he could wear over his contacts because they didn't change his vision. Chief Constanza was still in the station's foyer when Sid pulled the FBI ID with his alias from his suit pocket and approached the chief. It's easier for him to use the ID spontaneously because he can't get away with the wig and makeup routine that I can.

"Special Agent David Lawrence," Sid said, flipping open the ID case. "My partner and I would like to ask you a few questions about the Goetz murder."

Constanza cursed under his breath, but showed Sid and me into his office. The chairs in front of the cluttered wood desk were leather and well-used. Constanza's chair, also leather, creaked loudly as Constanza sank into it.

"What's your interest in this?" he asked Sid. He didn't sound cross, just tired.

"Something Van Blinn was working on." Sid offered a weak smile. "Unfortunately, it's top secret."

"That's what NBPD was saying."

"So why do you think the connection between the two murders is weak?" Sid asked.

Constanza winced. "Look, I don't want to get the guys over there in trouble. They're keeping as tight a lid on that one as they can. But they did confirm some information for me. Van Blinn was suffocated. Goetz had her head smashed in, probably on one of the lamp tables in the living room. There are two, and they have some sharp corners. Given the bruising on her shoulders and the fact that there are multiple wounds on the back of the head, it seems unlikely that she simply fell and hit her head. Van Blinn was killed in the middle of the night by someone who broke into the house. Goetz was killed in the middle of the day and by someone she probably knew, since there was no sign of a break-in, nor was there an alert from the security system. The housekeeper confirmed that she'd seen Goetz alive and well at lunchtime, when the housekeeper left to buy groceries."

I looked at Sid, then the chief. "Do you know what the connection was between Van Blinn and Mrs. Goetz?"

Constanza's eyes opened wide as he chuckled. "Yeah. Goetz was a former hooker who worked at a house Van Blinn favored when he was younger. We don't know if she serviced him or not, but according to the tip I got this morning, they definitely knew each other."

Another quick look shot between Sid and me. We were getting pretty sure the chief had talked to Fedders.

Constanza cleared his throat as the phone on his desk rang. We nodded, and he picked it up, then scribbled something on his desk pad with a chewed-on pencil.

"Got it. Thanks." He hung up and looked at us. "Another good reason why I don't think the two murders are connected. We picked up some latents on Goetz's furniture that don't belong to the vic or the housekeeper. Turns out they match some prints that were found in a hotel room in Malibu about six years ago, where a Hans Goetz was found suffocated to death."

Sid's eyebrows rose. "As in Tina's husband."

"Yeah." Constanza's chair creaked as he shifted in it. "The Sheriff's investigators told me at the time that they were looking at Mrs. Goetz, figuring she might have paid someone to kill her husband. It was pretty well known that she'd married him for his money, and he was running around on her. But when I questioned her with the Sheriff's guy, she looked like she was genuinely grieving, which doesn't make sense if she'd been behind his murder."

"Any reason she didn't do it?" Sid asked.

"She was at a bridge game with her friends that afternoon." The chair creaked again. "It was a regular game, which is why her husband chose that time to get in some playing around. Never did find the killer."

I looked over at Sid. His eyebrow flickered for a second, and I blinked, then he nodded and smiled at Constanza.

"I think that's everything for now," he said. We all got to our feet. "If we get anything we can share on Goetz, we'll be sure to contact you."

"We really appreciate you talking to us," I told Constanza as we shook hands.

He smiled briefly, and we left.

Once in Sid's Beemer, we headed toward the western part of Los Angeles, stopping as we went through the downtown area for lunch in the Chinatown neighborhood.

"Odds Goetz' murder involves one of the johns?" Sid asked me as we ate slippery shrimp and chicken lo mein.

"Probably better than average. I wonder if Karen has that ledger decoded yet."

"I'll give her a call. It's not like it was a priority job when I gave it to her."

We chit-chatted about other things, then got back in the car.

I was not looking forward to our next stop in the hills of Brentwood. We'd gotten the address earlier, and when Sid and I talked about it on the way to San Marino, we decided it might be easier to talk to Mrs. Brightman to see if we could find out where her husband was the night Van Blinn was killed.

On the way there, we came up with a scenario that did not involve the FBI. I had my blond wig with me, and I put it on before I got out of Sid's BMW. He waited in the car, watching for signs that Brightman might be there. We were both wired and quietly confirmed that we could each hear the other as I walked up the concrete path. I knocked on the gray-blue door of a white clapboard house. Mrs. Brightman answered. She was small and wearing a light blue velour running suit. Heavy makeup surrounded one of her eyes, and it looked a little puffy.

"Hi. I'm with The Bright Day Foundation," I told her. "I was given your name as someone who might like to work with us. We fund art centers around the county, helping them build their collections and set up exhibits."

"I've never heard of you." She swallowed nervously.

"You haven't?" I frowned. "How odd. You're on my list from our event the night of January eighteen. Wednesday, a little over a week ago."

"I— I was here."

"Could your husband have been there?"

"January eighteen? I don't know." She frowned. "He's often gone. I don't think he was home that night until very late. But I can't be sure. And please don't ask him."

My eyes narrowed. "Mrs. Brightman, is your husband hurting you?"

"He's fine." She slammed the door.

"Time to go home," said Sid's voice in my ear.

I turned back down the path to the street. "I think so."

When we got to the house, Sid got on the phone with Karen Bischorn, who was still working on the ledger. He gave her the names that Dr. Farber had given him, and Karen said that would help a lot.

In the meantime, I called as Agent Devereaux and got Brightman's secretary to tell me that Brightman had been in and out of his office the day before, but she thought he'd been in some time between noon and two. She didn't sound too anxious to say one way or another.

Then Sid called Dr. Farber and asked if anyone had been following her or harassing her.

"No. Why do you ask?" she said from the speakerphone.

"I don't know if you heard, but Tina Goetz was murdered yesterday," said Sid.

Farber cursed. "Have you told the police about Mason Brightman?"

"Not yet. We're more worried that someone may be looking for you."

"Well, I haven't seen anybody. But I'll sure be looking now. Thanks for letting me know."

Hannah Davis called a few minutes later, and Sid put it on the speaker.

"Sid, have you heard about Tina Goetz?" she asked, her voice soft and pleasant.

"Yeah, actually. I have. I was thinking of calling you. Any idea who might have killed her?"

"Not really. Like I said, Mom kept me pretty well insulated from the guys. But with this ledger thing getting out, I'm taking off. I'm due for a vacation, anyway. You found me, so someone else could, and I'm not taking any chances."

"It's better that you don't," Sid said.

They wished each other well and hung up. A few minutes later, Nick bounded through the front door with his usual exuberance.

"I'm home!" he hollered.

"We're in the office and it's safe," I called back.

It has happened that Nick has accidentally caught Sid and me, um, otherwise occupied, usually when he comes home when we don't expect him to. So Nick has learned to announce his presence quite loudly, and we have learned to let him know when there's a part of the house he might want to avoid.

Nick was all but bouncing when he came into the office.

"Mom! Can Josh, Darby, and me go skateboarding at the beach tomorrow? Josh says his mom will drive. Can we?"

Sid glared at his son. "Why do you always ask your mom?"

"I dunno," Nick replied.

"You could ask me, you know," Sid continued. "Or both of us. We're both here."

Nick shrugged. "Okay. Can I go skateboarding at the beach tomorrow, Mom?"

I put my hand over my mouth, trying not to laugh. One of the things I love about working with teens is that they are still learning social skills. I'll admit that I'm a little biased when it comes to my sweet guy. [A *little*?? Okay. I'm pretty biased in his favor, too. - SEH] But I have to concede that he wasn't the most socially astute person at that time in his life. Getting there, but not there yet.

I looked over at Sid. He looked at me and we both agreed.

"Sure," Sid said grumpily. "Please have Lety call us with the times and everything."

"Thanks!"

Nick hugged me, then went over to where his dad was sitting in his desk chair and kissed him on the top of his head. Definitely not there yet on the social skills. As he ran off to presumably call Darby and Josh, Sid looked at me.

"They grow out of this phase, right?" he asked.

I couldn't help it. "Stella tells me you did."

Sid let out his breath with an irritated grunt. I couldn't help giggling a little, which made Sid glare at me.

"Keep that up," he said. "I'll be talking to your parents soon enough."

"Okay." I put my hands up.

The problem is, I already know what a pain in the backside I was to my parents, and don't worry about others knowing it. Sid generally tries to keep a more refined image of himself. Once Stella and he reconciled after their estrangement, well, that refined thing went the way of all flesh. Stella enjoys tweaking Sid about the foibles of his youth.

We got the weekend off. I spent Saturday sewing, then after Mass and errands Sunday, we spent the day with Mae, Neil, and their kids.

Monday morning, I was hip deep in writing up a proposal, which was the assignment for my curriculum class, when Sid got a call. He immediately put on his headset and started typing on his computer keyboard. Being engrossed in my own work, I didn't pay attention.

Sid hung up and took his headset off.

"You got a second?" he asked.

I finished a sentence. "Now I do. What's up?"

"That was Karen. She got the ledger decoded. She said once she had the names we had, it came together pretty quickly." Sid sat back in his chair. "And all of the guys that Farber mentioned are in the ledger. I'm thinking of calling Fedders."

"Why him?"

"He's done a lot of groundwork on this already. He might be better able to figure out which of these guys are still alive and which aren't."

"Have Steve and Ray come up with anything on the names you gave them?" I turned from my computer to face Sid's desk.

"Not yet, but I could call them."

"Or I could." I frowned. "You know, Sid, I'm kind of wondering about Fedders. He doesn't seem like he'd have that much of a stake in this, but maybe we should check him out."

"He's too young to have killed Sheila."

"I know. But maybe he has a connection to the person who did. A father or an uncle."

Sid's eyebrows lifted. "It's possible, but it seems like a stretch."

"Weirder stuff has happened." Something we knew well from our own experiences.

"It's probably a good thing that I haven't given Fedders those names that Dr. Farber gave me." Sid shifted in his seat. "But here's an idea. What if I give Fedders the names that Karen decoded and give those names to Steve and Ray, too? That way, if Fedders conveniently forgets to check out someone, we might want to look more closely."

The phone rang, and Sid picked it up.

"Oh, crap," he said after listening a minute. "Are you there now?... Good. I'd stay away for the time being. The cops seem to have a handle on the murders, but I wouldn't take a chance..." Sid wrote something down. "Okay. Got it. Thanks for letting us know, and we'll stay in touch, too."

He hung up and blew out his breath.

"Well?" I asked.

"Hannah Davis' house got broken into over the weekend." Sid got up and began pacing. "The cops had left her a message on her answering machine. Apparently, the security company got the alert and scared the burglar off, then called LAPD. Davis had to come down to L.A. to file the report, and said the place looked like somebody was searching for something. She told them about her connection to Tina Goetz and to Van Blinn, and the detectives seemed interested. But she's staying out of town until further notice." Sid stopped pacing and stood still for a moment. "I just now thought. Jacob Van Blinn said that his brother was prone to hiding his notebooks, and that the cops didn't find the one he'd currently been writing in. Is it possible that the burglar was looking for the congressman's notebook?"

I thought it over. "That would make sense. That would mean Van Blinn was killed by someone who knew him and knew that he was going after the campaign donors or that he was looking for Sheila's killer."

"And we have both in Mason Brightman." Sid started pacing again. "But no way to verify whether there's an alibi or not."

"I could try leaning on him," I said. "But something tells me it's not going to do much good."

"I've got a better idea." Sid grinned. "Why don't I do some sniffing around on Brightman? I think I know of a couple of guys who might like to dish the dirt on him. Then, when I've got the goods, we'll have something we can pressure him with, and we'll both go in and lean on him that way."

"I like that idea." I grinned. "And I just thought of someone else we can lean on. Earl Manotti." I looked over at the computer. "How about I give him a call after lunch? I should be able to get this proposal done by then, and I'll be able to concentrate on Manotti."

But before I could finish my proposal, I thought of something else and called Esther.

"Two things," I told after putting the call on the speaker so Sid could hear, too. "Do you mind seeing if a Jay Fedders was on a flight from San Francisco that landed in New York last Wednesday morning?"

"No problem," Esther said. "Oh, and I found out that Marlon and Reba Wanzyck were definitely on a plane from Honolulu on January sixteen. There's no way they could have killed Congressman Van Blinn."

"Which was my second question." I looked over at Sid, who shrugged. "I suppose it's possible they paid someone to do it and were conveniently absent."

"I could check his bank accounts," Esther said.

"Let's hold off on that." I bit my lip. "If he's guilty, we won't be able to use that as evidence, and I'm thinking they're going to want to put him away."

"Okay," said Esther. "I'll call you about Fedders."

"Thanks."

I finished the proposal, but it made lunch late. Sid didn't seem to mind. He was on the phone talking to somebody I didn't know. It sounded like he and Sid had known each other from the days when Sid was still sleeping around. His contact said that Brightman was a rank jerk. [A rat bastard, which was ironic as hell given what a schmuck Les was. - SEH] Alas, there was little more.

After lunch, I called Manotti's office. The secretary got chatty, but said that he wasn't in.

"Oh. Do you know where he is?" I asked.

"At lunch right now, and then in meetings for the rest of the day. Say, aren't you that reporter who called a couple of weeks ago? What was your name? Devers?

"Linda Devereaux."

"Right. Right. Boy, he was not in a good mood that week."

"I guess he was pretty upset." I bit my lip. "I heard he went out of town overnight right after I called. I don't know what I said to him."

"He didn't go anywhere. Hasn't gone out of town since before Christmas."

"You sure?"

"Absolutely. I talk to his wife all the time, and she would have said something. She hates it when he travels."

"Okay. That's interesting. Listen. Why don't I hold off on leaving a message? I'm on a tight deadline, and if I can't talk to him today, then it won't help. Thanks anyway."

Sid was not terribly surprised that Manotti had lied to him about where he was the night of Van Blinn's murder. But there wasn't much to be made of that, so I went back to reading.

Darby and Nick came home together that afternoon. Sy dropped them off, chatted briefly with Sid, then took off to get dinner for himself and Stella. At dinner, Nick didn't eat much, and by bedtime, he was throwing up.

He agreed to set the intercom in his room so that Sid and I could hear it. Sid and I took turns running downstairs to help the boy when he threw up. Darby didn't get sick, and as both he and Nick had eaten pretty much the same things all day, we figured Nick had picked up a bug.

"I hope we don't get it," Sid sighed around four that morning as he got back into bed.

"We'll see." I yawned and tried to go back to sleep.

January 31, 1989

I spent the next morning on pins and needles. Not only was I praying that I wouldn't get Nick's bug, a member of my graduate committee was coming to observe my later section of Basic Comp. The observation was no big deal. Each of my committee members had visited one of my classes the semester before. But I have to confess, I was a little worried about Maggie.

I didn't think she would do anything. She'd been a decent student, although she was still annoyed that she hadn't gotten an A from me yet. She was acing her other class. I was just feeling uncomfortable about her being there, and I worked very hard at not letting her know that. I didn't want Dr. Carmichael to notice.

A tall, imposing woman with large horned-rim glasses and a somber face, Dr. Charmichael arrived a couple of minutes before class started. I checked in to see if she wanted to be introduced, and she didn't care. She may have looked solemn, but I'd found out that she was actually pretty easygoing.

I introduced her to the class. Maggie was there, but the least of my problems. Matt Handler decided to get smart with me about the next homework assignment. He looked fresh out of high school and was just insecure enough not to wear his letterman jacket.

I glared at him. "Your protest has been noted. But your grade is still dependent on getting it done. Now, class, as it says on your syllabus, we're going to continue our work on sentence structure by having a parsing derby today. Each row will make up a team, then send up a representative. I'll read a sentence. The representative will get three minutes to label the correct parts of the sentence. If the sentence is not correctly labeled at the end of those three minutes, the rep will sit down, and the next team member will get two minutes to fix it. If the labels are still not correct, that team member will sit down. There will be a new sentence with the same rules. At the end of class, the row with the most students still standing wins."

"What's the prize?" Matt demanded, a smirk on his handsome, square face.

I smiled at him. "Bragging rights."

"Then what's the point?" he snarled.

I walked over to where he was sitting. There was a very small, tiny part of me that almost, sort of, felt sorry for him. He'd picked the wrong teacher on the wrong day.

"Matt, you are entitled to your opinion," I said, my voice going cold and steely. "But if you continue to disrupt class and to challenge me, then you will leave this room and suffer the effect on your grade."

Matt swallowed, but shifted his broad shoulders. "And who's going to make me?"

"I will." I folded my arms.

"Yeah." He snorted. "You and what army?"

"I am an army," I said softly.

"I don't have to stay here," Matt said suddenly. He grabbed his books and scurried out of the room.

I turned and smiled at the rest of the class. "I'm sorry about that disturbance, class. Now, let's play our game."

One of the most common complaints about Basic Comp courses is that they're boring. And they are. I'm good at English grammar, but nobody would think that I'm a grammar freak from the way I speak. [Yes, they would. - SEH] So my goal isn't to get perfect rhetoric from my students. It's to get them to know how to write clearly and reasonably correctly so that people don't assume they're idiots. If I'm a tough grader, it's how they're going to learn. The teachers I learned the most from were the ones who made me work. That being said, nobody likes being made to work. So sometimes I try to lighten things up.

The competition was fun, and the students laughed as they tried to beat each other. But then Maggie got her turn to try the sentence - and I'd made it a good complex one - and aced the labeling on her first try. No one else came close. I grinned.

"That is perfect," I told her in front of everyone. "I'm impressed."

Maggie flushed a little. "Thanks."

As class ended, Maggie hung back. Dr. Carmichael got up from her seat and smiled.

"I have to say that was a good job," Dr. Carmichael told me as I gathered homework papers. "You handled a very difficult situation there."

I smiled weakly. "It's putting up a good front."

"Yours was magnificent." Carmichael chuckled. "I was almost afraid."

"I'm sorry," I gasped.

"No! You were firm. You were clear. And you established your authority with only your voice. That is not easy to do."

I shrugged. I did have an advantage in that I knew darned well I could have kicked Matt's butt without breathing heavily. But that's the part of my life that I can't acknowledge.

"Thank you, Dr. Carmichael," I said.

She swept out, and I went back to collecting papers.

"She's right, you know," Maggie said.

"Huh?" I looked up at her.

"You kinda scared me, too, when you took on Matt." Maggie grinned. "But I'm glad you did. He's a real jerk."

Um. She didn't say jerk.

"I just hope he doesn't file a complaint with the provost's office." I stuffed everything into my purse.

"Oh, he ain't gonna." Maggie laughed. "Boys like him don't want to admit they got beat by a woman." She looked at me. "So what grade did I get today?"

I smiled. "You earned your A."

"'Bout time." She sauntered out of the room.

I went to my car feeling both utterly stressed out and utterly thrilled at the same time. There is nothing like getting a real compliment from a teacher, which is why I made a point of telling Maggie in front of the whole class how impressed I was by her performance. And I'd also just gotten one.

But I also had a sick kid at home - he'd been resting all day and was eating a little, which I'd found out by calling Sid and Nick as I'd had a chance. There was a case that wasn't breaking, and oh, yeah, the mountain of reading and paperwork that wasn't getting done. Not to mention having to get tough with a student in a way that might just get me bounced out of my classroom on my ear.

I headed south toward Olympic, which sounds a little counter-intuitive when you consider that I was trying to get north and west to Beverly Hills. But Olympic is one of the better east/west routes in town, and usually even better than being on Interstate 10.

The dark of the growing dusk grew, and I switched on my headlights. I kept the radio off, preferring the quiet of my thoughts. But then my pager buzzed. I was stopped at a light, so I pulled it from my jeans' waistband.

Esther wanted me to call Priority One. I grabbed my car phone.

"It's me," I said when she picked up, my voice tense.

"We got a security alert from Stella's school," Esther said. "Someone broke in just now."

I didn't curse. It's not something I do. But I really wanted to.

"Can you tell from where?"

"The front door, less than a minute ago. I paged both you and Sid. Do you want me to send a guard?"

"No." I swallowed. "I'm pretty close. I'll get it."

My family complains a lot about how Sid and I drive. And we do push it with speeding and weaving in and out through traffic. But that day, I went beyond pushing it. I found a couple side streets and pushed my little Datsun pickup as fast as I could. Under normal circumstances, it should have taken around ten minutes to get to the school from where I was. I parked in front of the building in five.

I wasn't sure if Stella was inside the school, but I tucked my Smith and Wesson Model Thirteen revolver in the back of my jeans just in case. It's a big gun, so it wasn't the best fit, but better than being hobbled by my purse, and I wasn't going in unarmed.

The lights were on in the front of the storefront where the school was located. A dark figure had Stella by the throat. I ran as if all Hell's demons were after me and crashed through the door. It made enough noise to startle the figure dressed in a black jumpsuit with a black all-over ski mask on. Stella fell as the figure let go.

We faced off, then the figure jumped at me. I blocked two punches and landed another in the figure's midsection. There was a whoosh of air, but the figure pushed me away and ran.

Stella gagged from the floor nearby. I dropped to my knees next to her.

"Are you okay?" I asked.

She coughed. "Well enough." She coughed again. "How did you get him off of me?"

"Um. Martial arts classes. Sid and I work out that way a lot." I swallowed. "It's a great way to stay in shape."

"I will have to concede that."

I helped Stella to a seated position. She coughed again, but didn't look like she had been hurt that badly.

"What happened?" I asked.

"I was working on some accounts and other paperwork." She blinked. "I don't know how long that man had been here, but I heard a music stand go over and thought that wasn't right. So I came out here."

I looked around the room. Sheet music from the bins by the wall had been tossed all over.

"He came at me," Stella continued. "I tried fending him off with a music stand, but he got a hold of it, then got my neck. He wanted a notebook. Said Sheila's kid had it, and he wanted to know where Sid was."

The door crashed open again.

"Stella!" Sid hollered.

"You okay, Stella?" Darby asked, running up behind Sid. Both their faces were ash pale.

"Well enough." Stella swallowed. "Lisa scared the man off." She rolled over onto her hands and knees. "I'll be fine."

"Were you here alone?" Sid demanded.

"I had work to do."

I hovered as Stella slowly got to her feet.

"Why wasn't Sy here?" Sid yelled.

"He has his master class tonight."

Sy had been teaching the occasional special class in the area since Stella had moved to Los Angeles.

"Damn you!" Sid paced frenetically. "Did you even lock the door?"

"Yes. I did." She leaned against a piano, then sank onto the bench.

"Alright. You're coming home with me." Sid looked at me. "Lisa, you take Darby."

"I'll go with Lisa," Stella said firmly, her blue eyes blazing at Sid.

"Fine."

I think Stella knew what was coming. Her lips remained pressed together as I drove us to the house in Beverly Hills. Sid had gotten there first and checked on Nick, then sent Darby to his room. I checked on Nick, too. He was sleeping. I headed for the office.

"What the hell did you think you were doing?" Sid paced as Stella sat on the couch. "Somebody shot at you, for pity's sakes. Why didn't you take your work home with you before it got dark? Don't you get it? This person is trying to kill you and almost did, if those marks on your throat are any indication."

"He didn't succeed." Stella's mouth set as resolute as Sid's when he's in a stubborn mode.

"That's not the point!" Sid turned on her. "You took an unnecessary chance, and you almost got killed. Just because you didn't get it this time doesn't mean you'll survive the next time he tries."

"You don't have to assume the worst, Sid."

"Well, obviously, assuming the best worked in your favor tonight." Sid went back to pacing. "What is it with you? Do you want to die?"

"Of course not. That's nonsense."

"Not based on the way you're acting. You don't know self-defense. You won't carry a gun."

Stella lifted her chin. "I did well enough with that music stand."

"Until he got a hold of your throat." Sid looked away, his eyes blinking. "I don't want you hurt, Stella. That's what scares me about the way you're throwing caution to the wind. Don't you care enough about the people who love you to take care of yourself?" He looked at her. "Don't you care enough about me?"

"I—" Stella swallowed. "I care, Sid. I care enormously. I care more than I have ever cared about a human being in my life." She looked up at him. "You. Sy. And now Nick and the rest of the family. But my sister..."

"Alright." Sid held up his hands. "You're going to tell me about your sister. All of it. All of whatever it is that has you acting this way."

Stella almost made it to her feet. "I do not want that miserable mess a part of my life anymore. I am tired of it weighing me down. That's why I need to find out what happened. So I can put it away, back in the past where it belongs. And out of my life!"

"But it is a part of your life, and in a way, part of mine, too." Sid sank into his desk chair. "So don't keep this back from me. It's not helping either of us."

Stella looked over at me.

"It would be better to talk about it," I said softly, and sat down next to her on the couch.

Stella took a deep breath and nodded. "There was a fight. I didn't even tell Sy. But that last day. Sheila had told me in June that she would watch you, Sid. She said I should go back to teaching. So that summer, I'd gotten a job at PS Forty-One. I liked it. And for a couple of weeks, things worked well. I'd work during the day when Sheila was there. She'd work at night. Except that she didn't always watch you. I came home a couple of times, and your diaper hadn't been changed. You had the worst diaper rash for a while. Another time, she'd left you alone. Then she started talking about going away with someone. She wouldn't say who. But that last day." Stella choked a little. "She'd left you alone again, to get some cigarettes, she said. I couldn't take it anymore. I yelled at her. Told her that if she wasn't going to take more responsibility for her own son, then she should just get out and leave us alone." Stella's eyes closed. "She said that was exactly what she was going to do, and that she was going to take you with her. That she was going to give you a better life than I could because she was your real mother. I was just a lousy substitute for a real mother's love." Stella's arms went around her middle.

I reached over and held her. "Sheila went to work, as usual. When she didn't come back, I thought she'd run off with this man she'd been talking about. I was so happy, Sid. At last, I had you all to myself, and I could take care of you. There was a widow downstairs from our rooms who agreed to watch you during the day, when I'd be at school. She had already been that summer when I'd go work with a private student. I couldn't count on Sheila to be there. But then a policeman arrived. He'd gotten my name and address from a Jane Smith, the woman Sheila worked for." Stella closed her eyes again. "I had to identify Sheila's body. She was so beautiful, so still. I found some cash in Sheila's room and used it to bury her, then went on with my life." She looked at Sid. "With our lives. Only you wanted her. Well, I suspect you were more reacting to me, and that she was gone. But it was a month or more before you settled down."

Sid nodded. "Sy told me about how I reacted. I know it was just being a toddler. Still, I'm sorry about that."

"As if you could have understood what had happened." Stella took a deep breath. "But I was angry and probably still am. I was angry at Sheila, then I was angry at the police for not doing more to find out who had killed her." She shook her head. "I'm tired of being angry, Sid. I keep hoping that finding out about what happened to Sheila will help with that. It hasn't so far, but I keep hoping."

Sid shut his eyes, then looked up at the ceiling. "I understand about the anger. And that knowing what really happened is important. Still, I don't think knowing is going to stop the angry feelings. If anything, it might make them worse." He looked at her, the pain in his eyes flashing. "Honestly, Stella, I was angry for a lot of years. I hid it with the sleeping around. I pretended that I was content with my life. I even believed that I was. I gotta tell you, I didn't come close to getting away from it until well after I met Lisa. When I fell in love with her. That's how I learned that love is a real thing, and it's the only thing that can overcome being angry."

"That doesn't bode well for me," Stella grumbled.

I laughed softly. "Yes, it does. Stella, you love. You just don't realize it. I know it's hard when what you learned about love was actually about control and hurt. But it's not the words, per se. It's how you act. And you are very loving."

She laid her head on my shoulder. "Perhaps. It's no wonder Sid fell for you."

It was some minutes later, but we finally got up and got the dinner that Conchetta had left for us. Darby made a point of giving Stella a warm hug, then, after dinner, Stella went into Nick's room and sat with him for a bit.

February 1, 1989

Nick was well enough to go to school the next morning. I drove and got back to find Sid pacing in the office, the photo of Sheila in his hand.

"Are you okay?" I asked.

"She's still not real to me." He frowned and looked at the photo again. "My mother and she just isn't real. I don't know why, either." He sighed deeply, then slid the photo onto his desk and shoved it away. "It's getting serious. Stella's not safe after last night. We need to look at all the possible suspects and figure this one out."

I slumped into my desk chair and got out a legal pad from the side drawer in the desk.

"We've got confirmation that somebody is looking for Van Blinn's notebook," I said, unscrewing the cap to my fountain pen. "Stella told me that the person who attacked her wanted it. Said he knew Sheila's kid had it, but couldn't find him."

Sid's eyebrow lifted. "I told her..."

"We know you did." I glared at him. "But now is not the time. If the notebook is still missing, what are the odds it's still in the room where Van Blinn was staying?"

"Where else could it be? We know he kept it on him."

"Could Noah Taplin have gotten it?" I scribbled his name on the legal pad.

"That is an excellent question." Sid stopped pacing for a moment. "Could Taplin have killed Van Blinn?"

"Why?" I asked.

"The same reason we were investigating him. Somebody wanted him dealt with, only more finally."

"But how does that explain Tina Goetz and the attack on Stella and Hannah Davis?" I fiddled with the pen.

"The attacks on Stella and Hannah are probably related to the notebook, which means Taplin didn't find it in Van Blinn's room and is going after whoever might have it."

"But would he know you as Sheila's kid? Or even know why Sheila's kid might have the notebook?"

Sid grumbled a curse. "Taplin remains a possible."

"Just because you don't like him." I rolled my eyes. "So?"

"That's not very Christian, Sid."

"I'm not a Christian." He resumed pacing. "Who else? Jay Fedders."

"Did you find anything out from either him or Steve and Ray?"

"Ray called this morning. Allan Malfy is still around and living on Long Island. However, he was at a very well-publicized gala in New York the night Van Blinn was killed, and in his office all day when Tina Goetz was." Sid ticked off the next name on his forefinger. "Warren Halstead is dead, as is most of the other clients."

"Are most of the clients."

He shot me a glare. "The one guy that isn't dead is solidly alibied since he's in a convalescent home and not exactly all there."

"So I guess the question is whether or not Fedders has a connection to any of those men?" I drew a crooked box around Fedders' name. "We know he was on the West Coast when Van Blinn was killed. It was probably pretty easy to drive down here, then go right back up for whatever meetings he had."

Sid frowned. "There's something hinky about that. He said he'd come out for the Consumer Electronics Show."

"Wait a minute. That ended on..." I frowned and opened up our organizer. "Esther was there for her company, and the last day was the day school started, and you went to meet Van Blinn that first time. Yeah, the tenth. Van Blinn wasn't killed until the next week. Why was Fedders out here that late?"

"He said it was a big deal and that he was following up." Sid frowned. "But that does mean he could have killed Van Blinn. I wonder where he was when Goetz was killed. He could have flown out here after the funeral, but he was in his office when I called him that afternoon."

I made a note. "Something to find out. Who else should we be thinking about?"

Sid winced. "Paul West, but I talked to him as myself, trying to find out who killed Sheila. Why would I be asking about Van Blinn or Tina Goetz?"

"You think Sheila's killer got them." I suddenly grinned. "Maybe Special Agent Linda Devereaux should lean on him?"

Sid's grin grew evil. "That'll scare the pants off him, given what he does."

I made a note. "Speaking of scaring pants off people, what about Brightman? He's got a stake in both potential motives for killing Van Blinn and he's pretty cocky."

"True." Sid thought it over. "But is it possible his bravado is actually a front?"

"Well, if I had to, I'd swear that he's been hitting his wife."

"That only makes it more likely that he's all bluster. Still, Farber was pretty sure it was him. Maybe that was her way of pointing us in the right direction without saying it was him."

"We'll put him at the top of the list. And thanks to the notebook thing, that doesn't let Manotti off, either, and we know he's been pretty hinky."

Sid stopped pacing. "There's also the problem that Sheila and Goetz both had their heads smashed in. Stella was shot at and almost strangled. Van Blinn was smothered. That's a lot of different ways to kill someone. Could we be looking at multiple killers?"

"That is not outside the realm of possibility." I sighed deeply. "Which also opens up our suspect list, because if someone paid a killer or two, that would account for the different methods."

Sid cursed a blue streak, then stopped. "Okay." He took a deep breath. "Why don't we stay focused on our closest leads? What time is it? We can probably lean on Manotti, West, and Brightman today. Then tomorrow or Wednesday, we can go after Wanzyck."

"Why Wanzyck?"

"One, he's conspicuously alibied." Sid held up his forefinger. "Which would fit in with someone paying the actual killer or killers. Two, he can't have been happy about his mother-in-law being a former hooker, and if Van Blinn was about to blow that open, he'd have reason to keep the congressman quiet. Three, he'd have good reason to go after that notebook, and he'd be looking for it somewhere else because the cops didn't find it. And if that notebook is still in the room where Van Blinn was staying, then it is exceptionally well-hidden, because Wanzyck has access to the room and could search it himself."

"And if he didn't find it, he would be looking elsewhere for it." I frowned. "Do we have Esther pull up his bank accounts? It's not a legal search, so the evidence can't be used."

"Good point." Sid made a face.

Given that our jobs are more about finding out than putting people in jail, we don't always worry about whether or not what we turn up is usable in court.

"Let's focus on Manotti, West, and Brightman for today," I said. "We'll figure out something about Wanzyck tomorrow."

"Sounds good."

So I put on a nice pant suit that also made me look taller than I did wearing a jacket and skirt, then tucked my hair into a long black wig. I didn't pile on as much makeup as I do when I'm Linda Devereaux, but I used a different shade of blush and lipstick than my usual for Agent Diane Chapel. It's amazing how those little, subtle changes can really throw people off. Which is why I make them.

Sid and I went wired, and with him wearing his glasses, which was part of his David Lawrence persona. He hates how he looks in glasses, but has come to agree with me about those subtle changes.

We went first to Paul West's office in Brentwood, and somehow found parking on the street. Sid waited in the car. Upstairs, West oozed charm as he showed me into his personal space.

"How can I help you, Agent Chapel?" he asked, settling himself into his desk chair.

I slid into the leather chair in front of the desk.

"I assume you heard about Congressman Van Blinn's unfortunate death," I said, with a warmish smile.

"So very sad." West's face grew puzzled. "But that happened in Orange County."

"Nonetheless, there's a federal matter connected to the murder, so we're talking to the various people that the congressman knew to find out what we can."

"Sure. But I haven't seen the congressman in decades, like the early fifties or so."

"But as I understand it, you both were fond of a Sheila Hackbirn."

"I liked her. I knew her in Florida, and looked her up when I got to New York. But Tina was my favorite girl at that house."

"Oh. Have you heard?"

"Heard what?" West was surprised.

"That she was murdered last week."

"Nah. That's too bad." He still didn't seem all that grieved.

"And there was no competition between you and the congressman for Tina's affections?"

West rolled his eyes. "Van Blinn was bent on marrying Sheila. Can you believe that? What a mama's boy he was. Always writing in his notebook, talking about ethics."

"What were your feelings about Ms. Hackbirn?"

"I was sorry she got killed. I liked her, but sheez. She was a hooker. Big deal."

I looked at him sternly. "It is to her family."

"I suppose." West brightened a little. "Hey, I was talking to one of them a week or so ago. A Sid Hackbirn." He chuckled. "Have you talked to him?"

"Yes," I said, then looked West in the eyes. "He found it quite interesting that you claimed you could reduce his tax burden so significantly."

West jumped up. "Everything I do here is one hundred percent legal! I let you in here in a spirit of cooperation. You want to push me around, you'd better make it legal. Do you understand me?"

I got up slowly. "I understand perfectly, Mr. West. What you may not is that there is legally provable, and there is knowing. My case is about knowing, and I am reasonably certain that there is plenty worth knowing about you, legal or otherwise."

He came at me and was stopped when my fist landed in his chest.

"Don't." I glared at him, then smiled. "I'll let you alone for now. But be assured. We are watching, and we will be digging deeper."

I turned and left the office, Sid's laughter ringing in my ears.

"Well?" I said, getting into his car.

Sid leaned over the stick shift and gave me a big, sloppy kiss.

"You just get better and better, lover," he said, settling back into the driver's seat. "I heard him gasp. What did you do?"

"Just made sure he ran into my left fist when he came at me." I flexed my hand, which was feeling a little sore.

Sid laughed again. "Does he know you're right-handed?"

"Does it matter?"

Sid pulled out. "Maybe, maybe not. Let's do Brightman next. Maybe I can one-up you."

"That won't be too hard." I chuckled. "You are quite the man."

Sid's eyes glowed with delicious lust. "Ah, but, my sweet Lisa, you are quite the woman, and I can't tell you how much that excites me."

I let that one go because, frankly, it does not take much to get Sid excited. Or me, for that matter. Sadly, we had other work to do and would have to wait.

We went to Glendale next, and Brightman's office. I stayed downstairs and made like I was waiting for an appointment. Sid was promptly ushered into Brightman's office. Alas, all Brightman did was prove that he was all bluster.

"Agent Lawrence, good to meet you," his voice said in my ear. "Please, sit down. How can I help you?"

"I need to ask you a couple questions about a Tina Goetz."

There was the slight squeaking of leather.

"Never heard of her," Brightman said.

"Actually, you may have known her. She was an associate of Jane Smith's, and I believe you patronized Smith's house at one time."

"Lots of times." Brightman snorted. "Oh. Tina. What was her last name? Plaschky, I think. Nice girl. But I liked Sheila more. That Southern charm thing she had going, and damn, she was good in bed. But what's up with Tina?"

"She was murdered last week," Sid said.

"Murdered? Well, that's too bad." Brightman's voice was completely unconcerned. "Sad commentary, isn't it?

We're not safe anymore. But, hey, why are you here about that? That's not FBI jurisdiction."

"The murder isn't, but it is connected to a federal case. Sorry, I can't tell you more than that. The Van Blinn case is a part of it, though, and I understand you were an associate of his, as well."

"So what? I haven't done anything illegal."

"You donated to his campaign, and recently told a reporter that he was going to vote in your favor if he knew what was good for him."

Brightman laughed, but there was a tinge of nervousness there.

"You can't believe that. She was out to make me look bad. They do that, you know?"

"Some do." Sid's voice was a touch acerbic, although I had to believe that he was smiling. "But we've been told that the reason Congressman Van Blinn was here in Southern California was to make sure you and another donor knew that he was not going to bend to your wishes. Now, why would he think he needed to do that if you hadn't already tried?"

"Um. I got no idea. None whatsoever. Look. I believe in the political process. That's why I gave Jimmy some money. And I got a couple of friends of mine to donate, too. Why not?"

"Except that now Van Blinn is dead, as is another woman, both of whom you knew, one of them intimately."

"Look, I didn't have anything to do with any of that. I swear it!" Brightman's voice rose a little as the words came faster and faster. "So I gave some money to Van Blinn's campaign. That's no big deal. It's just the kinda man I am.

A real stand-up guy, and if anybody tells you different, he's lying. I mean that."

"Then you can share with me your whereabouts on the night of January eighteenth, and the day of January twenty-sixth."

"Yeah. Sure." There was a light phone ring. "Gwen. I need my calendar."

"Yes, Mr. Brightman."

Tense silence reigned until the door opened a minute later.

"Here you go, Mr. Brightman."

"Okay." There was a slight pause as Mr. Brightman presumably flipped pages. "January eighteen."

"Yes. He was found on the nineteenth."

"Ah. Here it is. I was with the wife at the Friends to Africa gala. We were there until almost eleven." Brightman chuckled. "I was so pooped, I was late to work the next day."

"And the twenty-sixth?"

"I was here. All day. See? Three meetings."

"I see." Sid's voice tightened as he got up. "Well, thank you for your cooperation, Mr. Brightman."

"That's me." Brightman sounded relieved. "A stand-up guy."

"Who hits his wife and bullies other women," I grumbled.

I tried not to gag as Brightman fawned over Sid all the way to the elevator. I also did not want to think about what would happen to his wife or his secretary when Sid was gone.

Once Sid got downstairs, we walked around the corner to the parking lot where the Beemer was. Sid waited until we were in our seats and putting on our seatbelts to sigh deeply.

"It is no fun browbeating somebody who cowers," he said, finally.

"That's because you're not a bully."

Sid started the engine, then turned around to back out. "Which makes me all the more proud of you for showing the asshole his place."

"I just hope it didn't result in his wife getting hurt."

"Sadly, we do not have any control over that." Sid shifted into Drive, then chuckled. "But, but, but, I think I know somebody we can call."

"Liz Warner?"

Sid's girlfriend from high school. As in an actual friend in addition to someone he had sex with.

"That's a great idea," I said. I frowned. "I just thought of two things. Mrs. Brightman. She was not very clear where Brightman was the night Van Blinn was killed."

"Which doesn't mean much if she's that scared of him."

"True. And there's the Friends to Africa. Weren't they the group that got their hands slapped not too long ago because ninety percent of the money they raised went to overhead and not famine relief?"

Sid chuckled. "I do believe they were. But what does that have to do with anything besides being something that Brightman would support?"

"Nothing." I shrugged. "It just figures. Still, he was nervous and fawning, but he wasn't that worried about what you thought of Van Blinn, and didn't even get it about Goetz. Neither was West."

"Have no idea what to think about that yet. On to Manotti."

That office was in downtown Los Angeles, in one of the new skyscrapers that had been built recently, across Fifth Street from the old Central Branch of the Los Angeles Public Library, still closed after the horrible fire they'd had about three years before.

Because Sid had talked to him in person as David Lawrence before, we were sent into the nicely appointed office almost immediately. Manotti was fairly tall, but stooped. His dark hair had come out of a bottle, and not even a good one. On the other hand, it looked good on TV. His hands moved constantly, wiping the sweat off his forehead, adjusting his suit, and fidgeting with the pens and pencils on his oak desk.

This was the most trusted banker in L.A.? I knew that Sid's and my cash assets were scattered among a host of different institutions, Sid being a firm believer in multiple baskets for our eggs. I couldn't remember off the top of my head which accounts we had where, but I fervently hoped we didn't have one with this guy's business. [We had one, but after talking to him the first time, I moved that account elsewhere. - SEH]

"Why are you here?" he asked nervously as Sid and I settled ourselves into the rosewood straight-back chairs upholstered with green leather. "I'm afraid, Agent Lawrence, I told you all I know about Congressman Van Blinn."

"But now there's been a second murder," Sid said calmly. "One that is possibly tied to the Van Blinn murder." He held his hands out. "You can understand why we might want to talk to you again."

"I— I don't know anything." Manotti blinked. "I think I don't."

"Then why did you lie to me about being out of town the night of January eighteenth?" Sid glared at him. "You didn't think we'd confirm that?"

"But..." Manotti gulped. "Okay. There's a good reason why I said that. It has nothing to do with Van Blinn. Mason Brightman. He's the one who got me to donate to Van Blinn's campaign. Said we'd have this guy by the—" He looked at me. "Well, we'd have him in our pockets. I didn't think so. I really didn't. But it would be nice to have someone on our side in Congress. Or would have been. Then the CIA got involved. An Agent Noah Taplin. He showed up after I talked to that reporter and again after you came by. I— I had to say something." Manotti sank into himself. "Oh, God. I am so screwed."

Sid was right. Browbeating someone who cowers is not in the least bit fun.

"Maybe not," I said as soothingly as I could. "And, yeah, hearing from the CIA is darned scary. But what would they want with you?"

"I don't know!" Manotti looked at both of us. "I mean, not really. It's the CIA. Why would they be telling me the truth?"

We had to agree with him on that one.

"So what did he say?" I said quietly.

"The first time, the agent wanted me to know that Van Blinn was being watched and wanted to know what he'd said to me. Only he hadn't. The congressman, I mean. He called and called, and I just did not want to return his messages. I did not want a record that I had talked to him. It would not be safe."

"I agree," I said. "What happened the second time this agent talked to you?"

"He wanted to know what I did about the murder. Only I didn't know anything. I swear, I don't!"

There was that little glance between Sid and me.

"We appreciate you being honest with us," Sid said, getting up. "I'm sure this has been very stressful for you."

"It has."

We left with soothing reassurances. We got down to the underground parking garage and felt the tail at the same time. Half a glance behind me and I saw a figure, overly furtive, dashing behind a pillar.

"Taplin?" Sid asked softly.

"More than likely."

"Good. I'm in the mood to ream someone's ass."

We split up at the end of the aisle to see who Taplin would follow. No surprise, he followed Sid, who led him to another corner of the garage away from his Beemer. I followed behind, just far enough away for Taplin not to worry. Assuming he saw me, which he didn't.

Sid suddenly turned on Taplin.

"Hey, Noah. Good to see you again." Sid's smile was anything but sincere.

"What the hell are you doing here?" Taplin snapped. "This is my case."

"Your case?" Sid's eyebrow quirked. "Whatever. My problem is that I've got a suspect who lied to me, and I had to check that out."

I slid up close behind Taplin. Sid kept his eyes off of me, but he knew I was there.

"Right." Taplin snorted. "I know what's really going on here. Your side took Van Blinn out and now you're trying to cover your ass."

"Are you sure about that?" Sid's grin was angry. "Seems to me it's your ass that needs covering. Some guy you're supposedly warning gets iced? Have to wonder if you did the icing."

Cursing, Taplin grabbed for his shoulder holster. I put the nose of my Model Thirteen into his neck. He froze. Sid slowly drew his own Model Thirteen.

"You know, Noah, we are supposedly on the same side," Sid said. "We could work together. Share information."

"It's my case and you know it." Taplin snapped. He glanced back at me. "Unlike you, I don't need my girlfriend to save my ass."

Sid laughed. "She's not my girlfriend. And you're right, I don't need her to save my ass. She's here, though. Why not?" He walked up to Taplin and put his face close to Taplin's ear. "But I'd be very careful messing with her. Trust me. She only looks harmless."

Sid drew back a little, and I backed off. We waited for Taplin to run as fast as he could to the stairwell, then hurried to Sid's Beemer.

February 2 – 4, 1989

The next morning, after we'd spent the night before going around and around on all the possibilities, Sid made me promise to stay focused on my school stuff. I would have kept that promise had I been able to. But my brain knew that I had missed something, though I couldn't have said what it was to save my life. And I was fervently praying that it wouldn't come down to that.

I was almost on autopilot as I taught my first section of Basic Comp. Nick visited between classes, which made me happy and did help me forget the case and infuriating Company agents. But as I went over the finer points of commas in my second section, I couldn't help noticing that Maggie seemed off. Not just off, but miserable.

I dismissed the class on time and nodded at Maggie to stay behind. It was easy. She could barely get up from her desk, so I sat down next to her.

"Maggie, are you alright?" I asked gently.

"No." She burst into tears. "It was just so embarrassing!"

"What?"

"My psych class. We were talking about psychopaths. And it's really about people who have no conscience. And Rosie Diamante had to go and say I was a psychopath because I kept coming on to her boyfriend. I told her I was only flirting and it didn't mean anything, and she said that proved it."

I sighed. "I'm sorry she hurt your feelings, Maggie."

"What's wrong with me, Lisa?"

"Well, if it's any help, if you were a psychopath, I don't think you'd be asking that question."

Maggie laughed a little through her tears. "But I mean it. I'm only flirting. I don't even want those silly men."

"It sure doesn't feel that way." I patted her arm. "I know you don't mean anything by it, but it's coming off like you mean business. Even Sid doesn't like it, and he loves to flirt."

"He is one nice bit of man."

"True. But you also went after my son, and he's only fifteen. Maggie, you don't have to go after every man you meet as if he's your last meal. You're good enough on your own."

"Am I?" She sniffed.

"Maggie, why did you leave South Florida?"

She swallowed. "I wanted to be something. I didn't want to be poor Maggie who couldn't get a man without pretending to be pregnant." She snorted. "The funny thing was, I was pregnant. And when I lost it, I was so glad. But Jed. He was devastated. He kept telling me we'd still get married and try again. We had to try again." Her head bowed. "I should never have gone through with it."

"Why did you?"

"Because that's what we women do. We go after a man, then hang on for dear life. That's the worst part of being around our folks, Lisa. If you're a woman, you ain't nothing without a man. Then you had to go and get a man with money." She shook her head. "Mama never let me hear the end of it. If that butch Lisa Wycherly could get herself a rich man, why couldn't I? I had to go and get Jed Samples. And when I said I'd cancel the wedding, she had a conniption for the ages. Even Jed Samples was better than nothing." Maggie stared straight ahead, not seeing. "I think that's when I realized that I didn't want a man. I wanted to make my own money. I didn't tell any of them back home that. I didn't tell anyone, even your mama, and I love Aunt Althea. She's the first person who made me feel like I could be smart."

"I've told you how smart I think you are. And I think you're smart enough to understand that what you were told about how men and women act with each other was pretty stupid."

"You can say that again." She looked at me. "But I've been acting this way all my life. How do I act different?"

I sighed. "I don't know, Maggie. I come from a different place than you did. All I know is to be myself. But my mama came from your people, and she doesn't act that way. Maybe she can help you sort it all out."

"Maybe." Maggie shrugged. "Your mama told me that she wanted to make something of herself, too. That's why she went to New York. She figured no one would want her to do that in South Florida."

"I know. She told me that, too."

I saw Nick's dark, wavy hair outside the classroom door.

"Why don't you call Mama tonight?" I told Maggie, then took a deep breath. "And why don't you come visit us sometime this month? We'll be having a family party on the twelfth for Nick's birthday."

"The whole family?" Maggie's face grew pained.

"Well, Mae and Neil and the kids, Mama and Daddy, Sy and Stella."

Maggie shook her head. "Lisa, I'm glad you asked. And I don't want to hurt Mae's feelings. She's been as nice as can be, inviting me to everything. But there's a reason I haven't been showing." She scrunched up her nose. "There's just too many little kids around, and even your teenagers give me the heebie-jeebies. It's too much like being at my sisters' houses. Screaming babies and mouthy brats. Yuck." She looked nervous. "Your boy is nice, and I don't mind being around him if it's just him. You know what I mean?"

I chuckled. "Yeah. I do. We can get pretty noisy. We'll just have to get you acclimated to us."

Maggie took off, and I collected my papers and Nick and headed home.

Nick asked about Maggie as he, Sid, Darby, and I ate dinner that night.

"She seemed pretty upset when I saw her in the classroom with you," Nick said.

"She got into trouble with one of her classmates over flirting with the boyfriend." I sighed.

"She is pretty predatory," Sid grumbled.

"She's a Man-Eater," Darby sang, laughing.

I glared at him. "You know that song is incredibly sexist."

"So?"

"How do you think that affects Maggie?" I growled. "She's expected to get a man any way she can, go after him, and hang onto him for dear life. But when she does, she's accused of being predatory. When men act that way, they're smooth operators. They're cool and sexy."

The boys' eyes landed on Sid, who shrugged.

"She's right," he said softly. "It isn't fair to women, and it does perpetuate the idea that it's okay for men to treat women badly, including hurting them physically and emotionally. Which is not okay in the least. Whatever crap I got into, it was always based on consent and with consideration for the woman's feelings." His eyes bore into the boys. "Are we clear?"

"Yes, sir," they each mumbled.

But as dinner went on, something nagged at me, and it wasn't Maggie's misery. As we finished eating, Sid had the boys put the dishes into the dishwasher and clean up what needed it. I nodded at the office.

"What?" he asked when we were alone.

"It's something Maggie said, about going after men and hanging on for dear life." I paced. "We've been operating under the premise that Sheila was killed by one of her johns."

"That would account for Jane Smith wanting to sell the house and get out of there," Sid said. He folded his arms as he thought. "But you're right. That's not necessarily the case."

"What if there was some rivalry going on between the women?" I asked. "Didn't Tina Goetz imply that there was?"

"It didn't sound like anything unusual."

"But what if something about it scared Jane Smith?" I frowned. "Or what if the reason Smith sold the house was that she really did have a movie deal waiting for her daughter?"

"Which would make her sudden departure more of a distraction than a clue."

"Right." I went back to pacing. "We know Goetz got killed. What if she was the one who killed Sheila, and someone else killed her in revenge?"

"That's possible." Sid shook his head. "Then why would the notebook be an issue? It seems more likely that Van Blinn caught onto something, and whether or not he wrote about it, whoever decided not to take the chance and killed him."

"Then killed Tina Goetz probably because Tina thought she knew who the killer was."

Sid nodded. "We need to get into that room and see if we can find that notebook."

We decided to go that night. There was no point in waiting. We had a good idea of the layout based on having been there and looking at it from the outside. Esther had a maintenance code for the house security system, which meant we could go in through the front and enter the code before it summoned the guards. We also had the gate code she'd gotten earlier in January.

We left around midnight, wearing black break-in pants, light-colored shirts, and black hooded zip-front sweat-shirts, our automatics in back waistband holsters. The boys were asleep, and, it turned out, never noticed that Sid and I had gone. We got to Orange County at about quarter 'til one and drove first around the back of the gated complex and checked for lights on in the Wanzyck house. All was dark.

We drove around front, used the code we had to get in through the gate, and parked in a neighbor's driveway, then walked down the dimly lit street. While there was a light on over the front door of the Wanzyck house, the door was largely obscured by all the bushes in front. I checked through the glass at the side of the front door.

"All dark," I whispered.

Sid nodded. We put on all-over knit ski caps, black leather gloves, and zipped up the fronts of our sweatshirts. Sid had the door open in less than a minute, and we slid inside. I punched in the code Esther had given me and held my breath. The alarm didn't sound. Nothing seemed to register.

We hurried to the back of the house where Van Blinn's room had been. A tiny bit of yellow police tape remained stuck to the door, next to the knob, but the rest of it was gone.

"Hm," hissed Sid softly.

I looked around. The other bedrooms had to be on the other side of the house, because what looked like the garage was the only other part of the house back that way.

We slid into the guest room, and I shut the door. We paused and listened. Silence. Sid pulled the blinds on the sliding glass door shut, then we started searching. Foregoing drawers and other obvious spots, we started with behind the furniture and in the back spaces of the closet. We had to assume the more obvious places had already been searched. There was nothing behind the dresser. I went into the bathroom, and used my penlight to comb the cupboards under the sink and even looked behind the toilet and inside the tank. I checked the shower/bathtub, then emptied the small linen closet in there, and put everything back.

Sid had the bed pulled out from the wall - no easy feat considering that he had to do it silently. The plush carpeting helped muffle us, but it wasn't guaranteed.

"Somebody has already gone over the bedside table," he whispered. "It's been moved. No sign of anything moved behind the bed, though. Wait. I was wrong." He flashed his penlight. "And here it is."

He pulled up the black notebook, then stashed it in his pants waistband, covering it with the sweatshirt. We moved the bed back into its original position. I looked again at the nightstand and gasped.

"Sid, that's the same one that was in Sheila's room."

"What?"

I pulled a small camera from one of the many pockets on my pants.

"It's the same style as the one in the crime scene photos in New York." I got the shot, and we both recoiled from the flash.

Sid paused, and we both listened again. Silence reigned. That, however, did not last long. As we headed to the front of the house, we heard faint humming. Grabbing my gun, I slid toward the living room, hugging the wall, Sid right behind me.

Wanzyck, wearing striped pajamas, wandered into the living room without turning on a light. I vaguely recognized the tune he was humming, but couldn't place it. It was some hymn, though. He wandered over to the couch, then knelt down next to it, lifting his hands in praise.

"Once again, Father, I lift up my hands to you," he said softly. "Taking comfort in praising you. Thanking you for the blessings you have bestowed on me. I have kept true to your word."

And he went on in that vein as I signaled Sid to go back down the hall toward the guest room. The was a door to the outside at the end of the hall and Sid opened it.

No alarm. Well, no wonder. It was off. We slid through. Sid slowly, agonizingly, shut the door, and we scrambled around toward the front, then through the gate to the driveway. After removing our masks and unzipping our sweatshirts, we walked back to the Beemer and got it out of the neighbor's driveway.

Sid cursed as we left the complex. "He really believes that crap."

"That just makes him a sincere hypocrite," I grumbled and made the sign of the Cross. "Have mercy on me, Lord, a sinner."

Sid chuckled, even though he knew I was serious. He'd recognized the parable I was quoting. Believe it or not, he's pretty on top of the Bible, and had been even before he knew me. He called it the best defense there was against Bible-thumping idiots. I always found it rather ironic that the Bible-thumpers that had wanted Sid to read the Bible had succeeded, only to have it totally backfire when Sid did not believe, as they expected, but threw the Bible right back in their faces.

The next morning, I drove the boys to school, then swung down to Baldwin Hills and Jesse and Kathy's house. Sid had called ahead, and they were expecting me. I gave Jesse the camera I'd had in my pocket the night before, and he took it straight to his dark room. I played with Keshon and chatted with Kathy as I waited.

It didn't take long. Jesse had made the print look as much like a police crime scene photo as possible. I thanked him and hurried back to Beverly Hills.

At home, Sid had the photos from Sheila's death on the desk. He looked at the print I had and cursed.

"That's got to be the same bedside table," he said. "Look. There's even the same ding on that one pillar."

"Well, I guess we know who killed Sheila," I said sadly.

"Yeah." Sid took a deep breath and looked away. "And probably who killed Van Blinn. In the last few pages of his notebook, he's worried about Earline. He wrote that she'd been getting more insistent that she deserved him more than Sheila did, that she loved him more than Sheila ever had. And the last entry, Earline told him that she'd even made sure that Sheila's bedside table was in his room, that's how much she loved him. And in the next line, he writes that he'll be leaving the next day."

I frowned. "But she's not that big."

"She's big enough."

"But she's got to be over sixty. How could she have smothered Van Blinn?"

"That's probably why she smothered him." Sid paced. "She would just need her weight on top of him. And her body isn't all aerobics. I'd be willing to bet she's done some strength training, too. For the toning."

I thought about it. "Goetz was probably not that strong, and being the same age, it would be a lot easier for Earline to smash her head in. But what about the man who attacked Stella?"

"Same thing with the age." Sid stopped pacing, and his eyebrows rose. "Earline has this deep, raspy voice. When she came after Stella, Stella assumed that it was a man attacking her, and the voice didn't contradict it."

"What about the shooting?"

Sid shrugged. "I have no idea. Even odds, she hated Stella on principle."

"We'll probably never know." I made a face. "And speaking of knowing, we now do know, at least about Van Blinn and Sheila. What do we do about it?"

"That is the question of the moment." Sid sank into his desk chair. "Stay the heck away from Stella?"

I laughed, then looked at the older crime scene photos.

"Sid, would it be worth talking to Jane Reilly about this?" I touched the print I'd had Jesse make. "I asked Jesse to make this look like a crime scene photo to better compare it to the old ones. But you know, we could say that someone just sent it in the mail to us."

Sid nodded. "That could work. What time is it?"

Sid called Reilly, and she couldn't wait to see the photo. Sid offered to overnight a copy. Which he did. The next day, we'd barely gotten in from our run at eight when Reilly called.

"That's gotta be the same nightstand," Reilly said from the speakerphone, her excitement ringing through. "Why don't I fly out there? I've got some vacation time coming. I'll bring some evidence bags with me. We know which corner hit the victim."

"We just have to figure out how to get in there," I said.

"Just ask," Reilly said. "You'd be surprised how often that gets you in. Especially if the people in the house don't think they're doing anything wrong."

So Sid and Reilly went back and forth on the arrangements over the course of several phone calls.

February 6 – 12, 1989

The soonest Reilly could get to Los Angeles was Monday morning. I went to pick her up from LAX, and we went straight to Newport Beach from there. Okay, we crawled a good chunk of the way. It was Interstate 405. Reilly just laughed.

"Sid called me when I was on the way to the airport," I told her. "He's confirmed that Mrs. Wanzyck is at home. He's following the Reverend around his office for the day."

Reilly giggled. "I can't believe the Rev fell for the whole doing a story on him line."

"Well, Sid is a freelance writer. That probably helped."

We'd determined that getting the Reverend out of the house would help with convincing Mrs. Wanzyck to let us into the guest room where Van Blinn had been killed. We weren't sure where Earline was, and decided we'd figure that out depending on what happened with Mrs. Wanzyck.

"You know, Dad had always thought there was something off about the Spinner broad," Reilly continued, referring to Earline by her maiden name. "He was looking at her at first. Then the brass told him to stop looking, and he had to figure one of the johns had stepped in, and it was probably the guy who killed Sheila."

Reilly's excitement was infectious. There she was, finally closing in on the case that had haunted her father until his death. The case that had inspired her to take up police work. It was exciting.

When we got to the gated community's gate, I said that I was going to Mrs. Wanzyck's, and they waved me through.

"Are you kidding?" Reilly asked me as I headed toward the house.

"I don't get it, either," I said.

"I'll take it." Reilly shook her head. "But if I lived here, I'd be raking those schmucks over the coals."

"I know. Sid said something about the residents getting pissy if their friends, maids, and gardeners have too much trouble getting in."

Reilly rolled her eyes. I took a chance and parked my little Datsun pickup on the street in front of the Wanzyck's house. I followed Reilly to the front door. It took almost a full minute after Reilly rang the bell for the door to open. Mrs. Wanzyck opened the door.

"Yes?" she asked.

Reilly flashed her badge. "Jane Reilly, N.Y.P.D.. I'm here following up on a tip regarding a cold case I've been following. It involves the murder of Congressman Van Blinn. I'm sure you'd like to get that resolved as quickly as possible. So would you mind showing us his room, please?"

At no time did Reilly pressure Mrs. Wanzyck, or tell her she had to cooperate. She encouraged cooperation, but in no way did she imply it was mandatory. I was impressed.

"Oh." Mrs. Wanzyck swallowed. "Oh. Of course. Please come in."

I followed Reilly into the house, fully convinced that the good detective could teach me a thing or two. Mrs.

Wanzyck took us straight back to the room. Instead of heading straight for the bedside table, which was what we were there for, Reilly walked slowly around the room, then into the bathroom. As she came back into the bedroom, her eyes swept the room, then as if by accident, they landed on the bedside table.

"Mrs. Wanzyck, how long have you had that little bedside cabinet?" Reilly asked.

"Oh, that ugly old thing." Mrs. Wanzyck shuddered, then rolled her eyes. "Since I was a baby. Maybe even before. My mother likes it. Not enough to keep it in her room, but she won't let go of it, either."

Reilly smiled. "I think there might be some evidence on that table. Do you mind if I try to collect it?"

"Of course not."

Reilly pulled a plastic bag and a box cutter from her suit coat, then squatted next to the corner of the bedside table. She held the bag under the corner and scraped away with the box cutter.

"Reba Wilson Wanzyck!" cried a deep, raspy voice. "What the hell did you think you were doing?"

Based on the description Sid had given me, the woman in the room's doorway had to be Earline Spinner Wilson.

"Mother," Mrs. Wanzyck said calmly. "She is a police officer, which means we are placed under her authority."

Oh, Lord, I hated that mindless subjection to whatever Powers That Be often touted by folks of the Wanzycks' mindset, never mind that the Scriptures are full of good guys flouting whatever authority in the name of God. Nor was I surprised when Earline didn't buy it either.

"You stupid girl!" Earline backhanded her daughter so hard, it sent Mrs. Wanzyck to the floor. Then Earline suddenly recovered and smiled at Reilly, who had stood up. "I'm so sorry, officer."

"Detective Jane Reilly, N.Y.P.D.," she said, smiling and pulling her badge from her jacket. "I'm just here as a courtesy. Obviously, I'm out of my jurisdiction."

I slid back toward the mirrored closet doors on the other side of the bed from the bedside table.

"Oh, of course." Earline smiled winningly, her voice still deep and dripping with sweetness. "But I do not understand why you'd be interested in that old bit of junk."

"It may be evidence," Reilly said, shrugging. Her hand slid under her jacket for a moment, and as I later figured, she was unsnapping the leather that held her sidearm in place. "Won't be able to say until we get this home. Odds are better than even it won't be worth much."

I swallowed. Mrs. Wanzyck had scurried into the hall. There wasn't much I could do. I was supposedly a civilian and needed to keep my cover as one intact. Still...

Earline sauntered over to Reilly, then suddenly punched the detective in the jaw. Stunned, Reilly fell.

"That is my bedside table," Earline growled. "It always was!"

That's when I saw what Earline had in her other hand. The automatic was not overly large, but in the close quarters, just as deadly. Reilly scrambled to her feet and tackled Earline, who fell back, beating her fists on Reilly's back. I edged around the bed, looking for an opportunity. I'd left my purse in the truck, so I didn't have my Model Thirteen and wouldn't have wanted to use it in that situation, anyway.

Then I saw it. Reilly's pistol had fallen out of its holster as she and Earline grappled. I grabbed it. Reilly shoved

Earline away, but Earline pointed her automatic at Reilly. I shot first.

Earline sank to the floor, her eyes open and staring without seeing. Reilly's gun fell from my hands, and I ran. The door at the end of the hall beckoned, and I burst through it, my stomach twisting thirty ways to Sunday. Once outside, I heaved.

I heaved again, spewing everything I'd eaten for the past three days into the bushes on the side of the house.

"It's okay," said a soft voice next to me.

I spat into the bushes and looked at her.

"It's okay," Reilly said again.

"She's dead," I whispered.

"Yeah. But you saved my life."

As if that was going to help. I heaved again. Reilly held my forehead and midsection, then pulled me close to her, rubbing the backs of her hands against mine to get at least some of the gunshot residue off my hands and onto hers.

"Don't worry. I'll take it." Reilly smiled at me. "It was clearly self-defense, and I won't get the heat you will."

Everything was a blur after that. Sid was suddenly there. I later learned that Mrs. Wanzyck had called her husband even before she called the Newport Beach Police.

I don't know when I got to go home, but Sid had made sure that Nick and Darby would stay with Stella. Reilly drove my truck to the house. Sid offered to let her stay with us, but she said no. I'm not sure why, nor did I care. Sid took me upstairs to our bedroom. He took out his contacts, then led me to the bed. And we spent that night making love over and over again.

It wasn't as much fun as that sounds. But making love is the most life-giving thing that we do. It didn't entirely help, but it was the best antidote to what I'd done that day. I was still a mess the next morning, so bad that I even cancelled my classes, something I almost never do. Sid took Reilly to the airport the next day.

Lillian called the Wednesday after everything happened. Noah Taplin had been reprimanded for screwing up the case, and was not happy. According to Lillian, he'd accused Sid and me of killing Van Blinn, which was so ridiculous even the higher-ups didn't believe him.

I don't suppose that we'll ever know what set Earline off that night she killed Sheila, but based on what we'd read in Van Blinn's notebook and what we'd heard from the other women, it was probably connected to the bedside table.

We ended up celebrating Nick's birthday in New York City, on February 10, the weekend after we'd caught Earline. His actual birthday is Valentine's Day, but that was in the middle of the following week that year. We'd planned to have the family party at home the weekend before that day. But when things fell out the way they did, Sid talked Nick and Mae into going to New York, which was not hard to do. Come to think of it, everyone liked the idea.

We flew to New York on Thursday. I'd canceled classes again, which did not make me happy, but I was still in no shape to be teaching. Sy and Stella flew with us, with the rest of the Fam-Damily coming on a later flight. We called Reilly shortly after we landed, and she agreed to meet us at the cemetery in Queens. We stopped first at a florist near the airport, where Stella bought a small pot of pink tulips.

Reilly hugged me especially tightly when we found her next to the small gravestone that read "Sheila Caponetti, August 12, 1930 - September 19, 1952."

"You okay?" Reilly asked.

I shrugged. "Getting there."

"I, uh, know you're a civilian but..." Reilly patted my shoulder. "When I was in your shoes a couple years ago, my brother, the shrink, dragged me kicking and screaming to a good trauma specialist. It helped a lot. Really."

I smiled softly. "So I've heard. I, uh, already have an appointment for next week."

Reilly hugged me again, then hugged Sid and Stella.

"I'm so glad you guys are here," Reilly said, her eyes blinking. "I can't tell you what it means to my whole family to put this one to bed."

"Is your father here?" Stella asked.

"Nah. Holy Cross in Brooklyn." She grinned at us. "And it wasn't just your sister's case that you guys helped clear up. I got word yesterday afternoon. The fingerprints they found in Tina Goetz's living room matched the ones they'd found in the hotel room where her husband was killed, and they matched Mrs. Wilson's."

"You mean Earline?" Stella asked.

"Yeah." Reilly shrugged. "We probably won't ever know why she went after Tina, but I'm willing to bet she was doing a favor for her friend when she killed old man Goetz."

My stomach turned, and Sid pulled me close to him.

"And NBPD did not give me any heat about the shooting," Reilly continued, nodding at the tombstone. "This case and those other two are officially closed."

Stella thanked Reilly, then looked at the gravestone. With a deep sigh, she put the pot of pink tulips on the grave. A minute later, we all walked away.

Sid made sure that Jacob Van Blinn got his brother's notebook. Jacob tried to give him some money, but Sid refused it.

Late that afternoon, we checked into the hotel where we would all be staying once everybody got in. It was a comfortable place, not far from Times Square.

As we got settled in our room, I looked over at Sid.

"How are you doing?" I asked.

"Pretty good." He stopped unpacking for a moment to think. "Actually, darned good. I know what's been bothering me. It wasn't Sheila. Yeah, it was weird getting a sense of who she was for the first time in my life. But I was thinking on the plane, even during that first lunch with Fedders. Yeah, I wanted to see what his game was before committing to anything. But as soon as Sheila's name came up, in the back of my skull was this one thought, 'What do I tell Stella? How do I tell Stella?' Then she went so flat when we saw the room. I'd never seen her that bad before, and it was pretty freaky. And after she went so crazy trying to find Sheila's killer." Sid shuddered. "And, yeah, there were the other feelings about Sheila and finding out about her. But almost exclusively, it was worrying about Stella. Trying to keep Stella alive and all that."

Shortly after that, we went to check on Sy and Stella. Stella was still off.

"I thought finding out what happened to Sheila would make me feel better," she told us, frowning, as we sat in a nearby coffee shop. "But I'm still angry at her. And I think I finally know why. She didn't care about you, Sid. The one thing I cared about more than anything in the world was you, and she didn't care. I think that's why I used to get so angry when you'd get all indifferent. It reminded me of Sheila and how indifferent she was."

Sid smiled and chuckled ruefully. "That makes sense. The funny thing is, as Lisa has pointed out to me any number of times, when I act indifferent, that's usually when I care the most."

Stella's eyes opened wide, and then she smiled. "Yes. I see that now." She shook her head. "I can't say the same of Sheila. But that is in the past. You're right, Sid. It will always be a part of me, and a part of you." She shook her head.

Sid winced, and Stella's eyebrow quirked up.

"She's still not very real to me," he said, looking guilty. "But I finally figured out why. She was not really my mother. You are, and always have been. You're the one I've been worrying about."

"Your mother. Hm." Stella nodded slowly, then she reached over and held Sid's hand. "I love you, Sid."

"I love you, too, Stella." Sid smiled.

Stella cleared her throat. "Now, what all did Nick want to do here?"

(Postscript/Sid's Voice)

In terms of the loose ends, I'm not sure what happened with the Wanzycks, although he stayed in his pulpit for a good many years. I was pretty disgusted when he spun his mother-in-law's death as the inevitable result of sinful behavior. He claimed she had turned from her sinful ways (which we knew she hadn't), yet dumped her past sins on her. All these years later, and Lisa still foams at the mouth if his name comes up.

Hannah Davis returned to her house and went back to work. I wouldn't say we're close friends, but we do socialize here and there. Jay Fedders, on the other hand, turned into a pretty good client for the writing biz. We lost touch with Rhoda Farber shortly after everything went down.

As for Earl Manotti, it turned out that he was so nervous for good reason. His S&L went under in March '89. Mason Brightman's chain of S&Ls got bought out a year later, and he made out like a bandit, which only proves that life is seldom fair.

Paul West also did okay, as far as I know. His claim that he might be the sperm donor who started me, well, that got disproved in 2014. My granddaughter, then 10 years old, convinced her dad to post his DNA sample to some website in the hopes of finding some of his siblings. Instead, Nick found a paternal aunt. Barbara is great, but her father, the actual sperm donor, was not so much. It turns out that Barb and I have a whole bunch of half-siblings, and we're still sorting out Barb's father's estate to take them into account. Nick does not appear to have any half-sibs, for which I am grateful.

I can't say that I was expecting Stella to say that she loved me that day in New York, but, yeah, it sure meant a lot. I had never thought she'd get that far, which only says how much love can do.

10:22 p.m.

3/31/24

Thank You for Reading

I do hope you enjoyed the book.

If you can do me one small favor, please. Can you go to one of the social media/retail profiles below and leave a short review? It doesn't need to be a lot, just honest.

amazon.com/Paths-Taken-Operation-Quickline-Book-ebook/dp/B0DGMYM7GB

bookbub.com/books/paths-not-taken-by-anne-louise-bannon

facebook.com/robingoodfellowent

goodreads.com/book/show/218688480-paths-not-taken?from_search=true&from_srp=true&qid=eCL2BChH7v&rank=1

Coming Soon

Believe it or not, **Necessary Chances** is the last Quickline novel. Don't panic. Sid and Lisa and the whole crew will be back with a new assignment. Eventually. In the meantime...

Christmas time is here. Not so much happiness and cheer.

The Christmas season may be Lisa Wycherly's favorite time of the year, but December 1989 is shaping up to be the worst ever.

First, her husband, Sid Hackbirn, gets the shock of his life when an old high school buddy turns up unexpectedly, triggering Sid's terrifying memories of fighting in the Vietnam War. Worse yet, the encounter pushes Sid and Lisa into investigating three crooked Federal agents while trying to hide their own top-secret work from their family and Sid's other friends.

But there's a family problem too. Lisa's nephew Darby may be heading for trouble thanks to his exceptional talent as a violinist. A persistent agent is courting the 16-year-old, as are any number of girls. With Darby determined to stand on his own two feet, the rest of the family is worried that the boy is about to get himself into the kind of trouble adults can't handle.

With Darby's ego spinning out of control, and each attempt to capture the crooked Feds going ever more disastrously awry, Lisa's merry little Christmas is turning into one deadly mess.

Other books by Anne Louise Bannon

I'm so glad you liked this book! Check out my other novels, available in print or ebook at your favorite retailer:

Old Los Angeles Series:
Death of the Zanjero
Death of the City Marshal
Death of the Chinese Field Hands
Death of an Heiress
Death of the Drunkard

Operation Quickline Series:
That Old Cloak and Dagger Routine
Stopleak
Deceptive Appearances
Fugue in a Minor Key
Sad Lisa
These Hallowed Halls
My Sweet Lisa
A Little Family Business
Just Because You're Paranoid
From This Day Forward
Silence in the Tortured Soul

Amateur Theatricals
Paths Not Taken
The Room Where it Happened

Freddie and Kathy Series:
Fascinating Rhythm
Bring Into Bondage
The Last Witnesses
Blood Red

Daria Barnes:
Rage Issues

Mrs. Sperling:
A Nose for a Niedeman

Brenda Finnegan:
Tyger, Tyger

Romantic Fiction:
White House Rhapsody

Fantasy and Science Fiction:
A Ring for a Second Chance
But World Enough and Time
Time Enough
And I would be honored if you left a review for this and any of my books on the below sites. It really helps.

BB bookbub.com/profile/anne-louise-bannon

goodreads.com/author/show/513383.Anne_Louise_Bannon

facebook.com/RobinGoodfellowEnt/

amazon.com/stores/author/B00JCRXST2?ingress=0&visitId=bfadb491-d1ac-4575-84da-bb4f7d325ad9&store_ref=ap_rdr&ref_=ap_rdr

pinterest.com/AnneLouiseBannon

instagram.com/annelouisebannon4/

Connect with Anne Louise Bannon

Thank you for sticking it out this long! Please join my newsletter. It's the best way to stay up-to-date on my upcoming projects, blog posts and even the occasional game and giveaway.

You can sign up for my newsletter on Substack, Substack.com/@annelouisebannon. or by visiting my website, annelouisebannon.com

And don't forget to connect with me on your favorite social media platforms:

BB bookbub.com/profile/anne-louise-bannon

g goodreads.com/author/show/513383.Anne_Louise _Bannon

f facebook.com/RobinGoodfellowEnt/

a amazon.com/stores/author/B00JCRXST2?ingress =0&visitId=bfadb491-d1ac-4575-84da-bb4f7d325a d9&store_ref=ap_rdr&ref_=ap_rdr

P pinterest.com/AnneLouiseBannon

○ instagram.com/annelouisebannon4/

About Anne Louise Bannon

Anne Louise Bannon is an author and journalist who wrote her first novel at age 15. Her journalistic work has appeared in Ladies' Home Journal, the Los Angeles Times, Wines and Vines, and in newspapers across the country. She was a TV critic for over 10 years, founded the YourFamilyViewer blog, and created the OddBallGrape.com wine education blog with her husband, Michael Holland. She is the co-author of Howdunit: Book of Poisons, with Serita Stevens, as well as author of the Freddie and Kathy mystery series, set in the 1920s, the Old Los Angeles series, set in 1870, and the Operation Quickline series, plus several stand alones. She and her husband live in Southern California with an assortment of critters.